Legacy of
Desire

Legacy of
Desire

MARINA
ANDERSON

sphere

SPHERE

First published in Great Britain in 1999 by Little, Brown and Company
This paperback edition published in 2012 by Sphere
Reprinted 2012, 2013 (twice)

A CIP catalogue record for this book
is available from the British Library.

ISBN 978-0-7515-5201-0

Typeset in Sabon by M Rules
Printed and bound in Great Britain by
Clays Ltd, St Ives plc

Papers used by Sphere are from well-managed forests
and other responsible sources.

MIX
Paper from
responsible sources
FSC
www.fsc.org FSC® C104740

Sphere
An imprint of
Little, Brown Book Group
100 Victoria Embankment
London EC4Y 0DY

An Hachette UK Company
www.hachette.co.uk

www.littlebrown.co.uk

Legacy of
Desire

Chapter One

Davina looked critically at the drawing in front of her and sighed. Something was not quite right about it, but she couldn't make out where the fault lay. There was no doubt it was erotic, and she was pleased with the air of urgency; the couple's embrace was desperate in its haste, yet still it lacked something.

Realising that the studio was growing dark she glanced at her watch and saw with surprise that it was already six-thirty. She was having dinner with her uncle in the main house at seven o'clock, which only gave her half an hour to shower and change. Switching off the lamp over her drawing board she left the studio and walked through the wooden door into her cottage, set in the grounds of her uncle's country house in Oxfordshire.

She enjoyed her work as a freelance illustrator, and the studio that her uncle had allowed her to have built was better than anything she'd ever dreamed of having when she was married. Normally she was very content with her life, but for some reason the drawing she'd just been working on, commissioned for a science-fiction fantasy novel, was making her feel discontented, as though she was missing out on something, which was ridiculous because her life couldn't have been better.

After her divorce, which hadn't been in the least bit amicable, she'd spent months in a series of unpleasant lodgings, and when she'd first come to Oxfordshire it had seemed like heaven. Used to the company of older people, having been brought up by her grandparents after her unmarried mother died in childbirth, Davina wasn't bothered that her main companion was a fifty-eight-year-old academic bachelor, whose only interests apart from his work were hunting and shooting. She loved her Uncle David, and since meeting Phil eighteen months earlier had thought she was completely fulfilled. She didn't mind the fact that Phil worked as an estate agent in London because she enjoyed having the weeks to herself, and most weekends he made the trip to Oxfordshire to join her.

At seven o'clock precisely, her short, dark, curly hair still slightly damp, Davina lifted the heavy brass knocker on the front door of the main house and brought it down heavily. Almost immediately her uncle's valet opened the door.

'Good evening, Mrs Fletcher.'

Davina smiled. 'Good evening, Clive. I hope I'm not late.'

'Exactly on time, as usual,' he replied. 'Your uncle's waiting in the study. Would you care for a sherry?'

Davina nodded. 'That would be lovely.'

In the study, the once bright carpet and curtains now faded with age, her uncle stood waiting. He had a mass of thick grey hair, and although tall, was slightly stooped due to too many hours spent poring over books. Nevertheless, he was a good-looking man and it always surprised Davina that he'd never married. He kissed her warmly on the cheek. 'How's the work going?'

'I think it's all right.'

Her uncle gave her a quick glance of surprise. 'You don't sound too sure.'

'I'm not,' she admitted. 'Technically it's correct, but compared with the manuscript my pictures lack something. The problem is, I don't know what.'

'Perhaps I should come and have a look,' suggested her uncle.

Davina shook her head. 'They're not your sort of thing at all.'

He smiled. 'That sounds interesting. I take it these aren't your normal run-of-the-mill drawings?'

'They're more ... adult,' said Davina, and to her annoyance felt her cheeks redden.

Her uncle laughed. 'I do have a bit of experience of the world you know, Davina. There's no need to protect me. In fact, I'd say that you're the one who needs to know more about life.'

'How can you say that?' she asked in surprise. 'I'm a divorced woman, or had you forgotten?'

'I hadn't forgotten. If you've finished your sherry let's go through to dinner.'

As usual the food was perfect. Davina's Uncle David

had had the same chef for the past ten years, and always said that he didn't know what he'd do if he left. Certainly Davina loved eating at the main house, especially since her normal diet consisted of instant meals thrown in the microwave, or tins of soup heated and eaten with rolls or bread.

'I worry about you, you know,' her uncle remarked suddenly.

Davina raised her head. 'Why?'

'You're only twenty-five, this isn't the life for you.'

'It's the kind of life I want,' she said firmly, trying to push her earlier feelings of unease to one side as doubts again began to assail her. 'Getting divorced from Michael was quite enough excitement for several years.'

'You should never have married him in the first place. How old was he?'

'You know perfectly well how old he was.'

'Quite, he was forty and you were nineteen. In my opinion it's because you never knew your father. Michael was filling the gap, but of course it didn't work out because he didn't want to behave like a father towards you, and quite right too.'

Davina shifted uneasily in her seat. Normally her

5

uncle never touched on personal topics and she found the conversation very awkward. She was an intensely private person and had always thought that she and her uncle were alike. 'What's this about?' she muttered.

'As I said, I'm worried. You've buried yourself in the middle of nowhere, with no young people around you, and spend most of your time shut in that studio drawing pictures for works of fiction. You're not living at all, Davina. You're simply existing or, and this may be worse, you're trying to hide.'

'Hide from what?'

Her uncle sighed. 'I've no idea. The true you perhaps?'

'I do have Phil.'

Her uncle pulled a face.

'I thought you liked Phil!' she exclaimed.

'He isn't exactly a charmer. He can be quite arrogant at times.'

Davina knew this was true. 'He doesn't mean it. He lacks tact, that's all,' she said defensively.

'You deserve better. Besides, he's an estate agent.' Their eyes met and Davina couldn't help laughing.

'Someone has to go out with estate agents.'

Her uncle nodded. 'Agreed, but does it have to be you?'

'Perhaps I'm in love with him.'

Her uncle's face became very still. 'Are you?'

'I don't think I want to answer that,' she retorted, her appetite fading rapidly.

'Which means you're not.'

'He suits me,' she explained. 'He's not here all the week, which I like and he's ...'

'Safe,' her uncle concluded. 'Safe, if a little boorish.'

'All right, he's not perfect,' conceded Davina. 'But who is?'

Her uncle didn't reply until Clive had removed their empty plates and served dessert. Then he continued the discussion. 'You're too young to settle for this, Davina. Your loyalty to Phil is misplaced. Before you know it you'll be my age and regretting all the years that you wasted.'

'Is that what this is about?' asked Davina. 'You've been sitting here brooding about your wasted youth, have you?'

Her uncle shook his head. 'I certainly haven't. It might surprise you to learn that I didn't waste my youth. I lived it to the full and although I made mistakes, when I look back now I don't regret any of it. You know what they say, a man who doesn't make mistakes doesn't make anything.'

'My marriage was my mistake,' retorted Davina. 'I'm not in a hurry to make another one.'

'You're a beautiful young woman,' said her uncle. 'Sometimes I don't think you realise how attractive you are. Have you thought about moving back to London now that you're getting established? You'd meet more people there and . . .'

'I don't want to meet more people,' she said shortly. 'Do you think we could talk about something else?'

'I feel responsible for you,' explained her uncle. 'When your mother died I should have taken more interest in your upbringing but . . .'

'But you were too busy gadding around, living life to the full,' said Davina with a laugh.

He nodded. 'Something like that. Anyway, I feel that the least I can do now is make up for my lack of interest earlier.'

'You've done that by giving me a home here. I'm really happy and just because I'm not living the kind of life you think I should be living, that doesn't alter things. Tell me one thing that I don't have here that I could find in London?'

Her uncle didn't hesitate. 'Passion,' he said curtly.

Davina stared at him in surprise. 'Passion?'

'Yes. There's no passion in your life, Davina.'

'That's it!' said Davina, suddenly realising the problem with her drawings. 'Thank you, Uncle, you've solved it for me.'

'Solved what?'

'Now I know what's wrong with my drawings. They lack passion.'

'How surprising,' he said dryly.

'What do you mean?'

'You can hardly put passion in your drawings when you don't know anything about it.'

'I do know about passion,' she retorted.

'Really?'

Davina thought for a moment. The truth was that she didn't. There'd been no passion in her marriage, and if passion was what she read about in books then there was none between her and Phil; personally she thought that passion was probably vastly overrated. In

9

any case, it was bound to lead to problems and she liked an easy, uncomplicated life. 'I'm perfectly happy. And although I may only be twenty-five I'm old enough to know my own mind. You must stop meddling in my life and get on with your own.'

'Point taken,' he agreed. 'But promise me you'll at least think about what I've said.'

'All right,' she conceded. 'Now, have you got any work for me?'

'Quite a bit. I'll give it to you after we've had coffee.'

Davina was relieved. Her uncle refused to take any rent for the cottage, saying that he didn't need the money. However, in order that she shouldn't feel beholden to him, she did all his secretarial work and also acted as hostess whenever he entertained.

At the end of the evening he handed her a folder full of typing. 'You haven't forgotten that I've got a shooting party coming tomorrow, have you?'

Davina shook her head. 'Of course not. How many will there be for dinner?'

'Sixteen.'

'Does that include me?'

Her uncle smiled. 'Naturally it includes you. I want

you to dress up in all your finery and play the hostess. It's eight-thirty for nine. Even you can't work later than that.'

'No I don't, it gets too dark.'

At ten-thirty she made her way back to the cottage, but although she went straight to bed she found that the conversation with her uncle had disturbed her more than she'd realised. She couldn't help wondering if he was right, if she was missing something. The problem was that she was afraid of taking risks. During her childhood her grandparents had been incredibly protective, terrified that, having lost their only daughter, they would somehow lose their grandchild as well. As a result, she saw life as being full of hidden dangers.

Men had been a taboo subject during her formative years which was, she supposed, why both her husband and Phil were such 'safe' men. Not that she'd met many dangerous ones, she thought to herself, as she drifted off to sleep.

That night, to her shame, her dreams were incredibly sensual. Davina went from one sexual encounter to another, finding intense satisfaction with each liaison, yet strangely all the men were faceless and none spoke.

When she awoke the next morning, instead of feeling refreshed she felt exhausted but at the same time on edge. 'Uncle David,' she muttered. 'What have you done?'

She knew she'd be busy all that evening helping her uncle entertain his guests, so Davina got down to work quickly. Looking carefully at her drawings she knew that what she'd suspected during her conversation with her uncle was true. Technically the drawings were very good, conveying the urgent, hedonistic desires of the aliens portrayed in the book, but technique alone wasn't enough. She knew now that the work lacked passion. In the novel the entire alien civilisation crumbled, destroyed by physical passions that overrode everything, including the necessity for some of them to quit their planet in search of inter-galactic assistance. The problem was, how could she convey this emotion in her drawings?

It seemed to Davina that now she had noticed the flaw in her work it was obvious in every drawing she'd done, where before she'd been pleased with the work. 'Why did he have to talk to me about passion?' she said with a sigh. It had been so unlike him. Even now she couldn't understand why he'd felt the necessity to address such a personal matter when their relationship, whilst close, had always been governed by certain unspoken rules, including lack of intrusion into each other's private lives.

At one o'clock she decided to take a short break and was cutting a slice of cheese in the kitchen when she heard a knock on her front door. She frowned. She never had visitors in the week and couldn't imagine who it was, unless Clive had some query that he was relaying from the chef. When she opened the front door it wasn't Clive standing there, but a man she'd never met before. His face was ashen.

'Are you Davina Fletcher?' he asked quietly. Davina nodded. 'My name's George Middleton. I'm one of your uncle's friends from the shooting party. I think I'd better come in.'

Puzzled, Davina stood to one side. 'Is something wrong?'

'I'm afraid there is.'

'Has there been an accident?'

George nodded. 'It was so sudden ...' His voice tailed off.

Davina felt fear rise in her throat. 'What was? Has something happened to my uncle?' George nodded. 'Has he been hurt?'

'It's worse than that I'm afraid.'

Davina began to tremble. 'You mean ... ?' She couldn't bring herself to say the words aloud.

'I'm very sorry, Davina, but your uncle's been killed.'

Davina felt as though she were standing back from the scene, watching herself as her legs crumbled and the stranger helped her into a chair. 'I'll get you a glass of water,' he muttered, hurrying to the kitchen while she remained seated, feeling sick and shaking violently from head to toe. He handed her the water and her teeth chattered against the rim of the glass. 'How did it happen?'

'He tripped over a tree root and his gun went off. It killed him instantly. He wouldn't have known a thing.'

His words conjured up a terrible image of her beloved Uncle David, and suddenly Davina began to cry, terrible tearing sobs that she was totally unable to control. 'Is there anyone I can ring?' asked George. 'A relation, or a boyfriend perhaps?'

Between sobs Davina managed to give him Phil's

number and then, realising that the main house was now full of guests without a host she looked up at her visitor. 'Where is everyone?'

'We're all at the house. Naturally we've called a doctor and an ambulance.'

'Give me fifteen minutes and I'll be there.'

'Are you sure? You don't look up to it.'

'I owe it to Uncle David,' she said simply. 'Now if you don't mind I'd like to be alone for a few minutes.'

Later, when she looked back on it all, Davina never knew how she managed to pull herself together sufficiently to go to the main house and mingle with her late uncle's friends, trying to utter words of comfort and reassurance to people when all she wanted was the same for herself. However, duty and manners had been instilled into her at an early age and she knew that her uncle would have wanted her to do the right thing.

It was only when it was all over, her uncle's body removed to the morgue and the visitors gone that she allowed herself to break down once more. Clive looked after her until Phil finally arrived, having left his London office the moment he received the telephone call.

'You look a little better now,' said Phil encouragingly as Davina listlessly ate a plate of scrambled eggs that he'd prepared for her. 'Have a glass of red wine, it will bring the colour back into your cheeks.'

'Don't be ridiculous,' said Davina. 'I'm pale because Uncle David's dead. Red wine isn't going to change that.'

'Of course not,' said Phil, and she could tell that he was startled by her unusual sharpness. 'Just the same, you've got to take care of yourself, Davina. After all, everything's yours now.'

Davina looked at him in bewilderment. 'What do you mean everything's mine?'

'Exactly what I say. The house, the estate, it will all go to you, won't it?'

'I've never thought about it.'

'You must have known that it would be yours one day, although naturally you wouldn't have expected it to be this soon,' said Phil.

Davina shook her head. 'I can't believe we're talking like this. Uncle David's been killed and all you're interested in is what I'm going to gain from it. Is that why you've been coming down here every weekend? To make sure that my future inheritance was being well looked after?'

Phil gave a nervous laugh. 'Don't be ridiculous, Davina.'

'But you had thought about it?'

'Naturally. Anyone could tell that your uncle was grooming you to take over the reins. I half expected him to move abroad in about ten years' time, especially after he started getting arthritis. He'd have been better off in a warmer climate, and you'd have been here to take care of things for him.'

'Well, he didn't live that long, did he,' said Davina, her eyes filling with tears.

Phil put an arm around her, but despite her need for comfort Davina stiffened beneath his touch. The rather unpleasant and totally unexpected mercenary streak he'd revealed had shaken her to the core.

'You need to sleep.' Phil's voice was soothing. 'You go on up now and I'll join you when I've tidied things away.'

She was too exhausted by the emotions of the day to argue, but when he finally climbed into bed beside her and she felt him snuggle against her back, his erection nudging between the cheeks of her bottom, she twisted away from him. 'How can you, Phil? You can't imagine that I'm in the mood for sex.'

'I thought you might like some comfort.'

'Just hold me,' she murmured.

'Sometimes I think that's all you ever really want,' muttered Phil.

Davina ignored him. She wondered why it was that tragedy was said to bring out the best in people. It certainly wasn't bringing out the best in Phil.

The following Wednesday, six days after his death, David Wilson's funeral was held. It was a beautiful August day and the local church was packed. Davina and Phil travelled alone in the black car that followed the hearse and Davina, dressed in a short-sleeved tailored grey dress and matching jacket, wished that it was all over. Her uncle wouldn't have wanted her to be so upset, she knew that, but it seemed extraordinary that he should die so suddenly, and so soon after their first truly meaningful conversation. It had etched his words even more firmly on her mind, and she realised that this was partly why she had found Phil so irritating over the past week. Uncle David had been right – there was no passion between her and Phil, yet she still felt she needed the security he offered.

'A good turn-out,' Phil muttered, as he walked down the centre aisle behind the coffin.

Davina thought he was making it sound like a local fête rather than a funeral, but he did have a point. Every pew was full and when she glanced around her she saw familiar faces everywhere, both local people and her uncle's friends, some of whom had flown in from distant parts of the world. As she took her place in the front right-hand pew she noticed a man who looked to be in his mid-thirties standing at the end of the row opposite. He stood out because, as far as she could tell, he was the only stranger present. In addition, he was very tall and stood extremely straight, while his brown hair was cut surprisingly short. Even at this moment of sorrow Davina noticed how well the hair had been shaped into the nape of his neck, and as she glanced away she felt a strange sensation in her stomach.

The service was excellent, everything Davina had asked for and more, with contributions from long-standing friends. When it was over she and Phil shook

hands with everyone as they left, swapping polite condolences and regrets. 'How many more?' asked Phil as
people continued to pour out of the church.

'I don't know. He had a lot of friends. I think it's
nice,' said Davina.

'Well, when they've gone remember we're due back
at the main house.'

'I know, I've laid on food for everyone.'

'And the will's going to be read,' Phil reminded her.

The will, Davina thought to herself. It was strange to
realise that very soon all this would legally be hers, and
even stranger to realise that Phil was more excited
about it than she was.

It was early afternoon before the last of the mourn-
ers had left the house and Davina and Phil were invited
by Mr Morrison, David Wilson's solicitor, to join him
in the study. On entering the room Davina was astonished to see the tall man she'd noticed earlier in church
standing by the mantelpiece. Since she was five-foot-ten
herself, Davina was very aware of a man's height. She
thought that this man must be at least six-foot-two; he
was rangy and strong featured, with an extremely conventional appearance. His suit was impeccably tailored,

his shoes polished so hard that she was certain she'd be able to see her reflection in them, but when he turned to look at her and she smiled in greeting his features remained impassive, leaving her feeling awkward.

'Davina, do you know Jay Prescott?' asked Mr Morrison, gesturing towards the stranger.

'No.'

'Jay was your uncle's godson. He's from Boston, Massachusetts.'

'I didn't know my uncle had a godson.'

'I didn't know he had a niece,' said the American.

For a few seconds the couple stared at each other and Davina was the first to avert her gaze. He looked like a man who was used to getting his own way and his presence dominated the room.

'Why is he here?' Phil whispered in Davina's ear.

She shrugged. 'I've no idea.'

'Well, now you've been introduced you'd better all sit down,' said Mr Morrison, looking slightly flustered. 'Your uncle drew up this will only six months ago. One might almost wonder if he'd had some premonition of this terrible tragedy.'

Davina felt a lump in her throat and swallowed

hard. Perhaps he had had a premonition, she thought; maybe that was why he'd talked to her the way he had. Mr Morrison cleared his throat. 'The will is extremely straightforward. David has left everything to his godson, Jay.' Davina heard Phil's sharp intake of breath but strangely she felt nothing at all upon hearing the words. It was as though her uncle's death had left her numb, and in any case she'd never thought about owning the house. But there was the cottage, and now her heart began to race as she realised that she would soon be homeless and without her beloved studio.

'However,' the solicitor continued, 'there is a clause in the will stating that "my niece Davina Fletcher must be allowed to stay on in her cottage for as long as she wishes, rent free, in return for carrying out any services that Jay Prescott may require while he is living or staying at the main house".'

'What a bloody nerve,' said Phil, no longer bothering to keep his voice down.

'Sshh,' hissed Davina.

'But you've been living here for years!' exclaimed Phil. 'We never even knew he had a godson.'

'It's none of your business,' she said. 'For goodness sake be quiet.'

'Quite an interesting little clause,' murmured Jay Prescott.

Davina turned towards him. 'Excuse me?'

'The wording of the clause. Didn't you find it interesting?'

'Not really. It's exactly the same terms I had with my uncle.'

'Surely not.' For a moment the flicker of a smile lifted the corners of the American's mouth.

Davina felt confused. 'Yes it is. I used to do all his secretarial work and act as hostess for him at his parties. Not that I suppose you'll be living here very much.'

'Why do you say that?'

'Because you live in America.'

'Yeah, but it just so happens that I'm due to spend twelve months in England on an exchange visit. I'm a public prosecutor you see, and I'm coming over here to learn a bit about English law. The house should prove pretty useful to me. I'll also be entertaining a great deal, and since I'm single I'll need quite a lotta help in that direction ...'

'That's lucky,' said Davina weakly, wondering what on earth had possessed her uncle to hand everything over to a man like this. 'At least I'll feel I'm earning my keep.'

'Believe me, honey, you'll more than earn your keep. I can think of quite a lotta other services I'll require from you, but as long as you carry them out in a satisfactory fashion I don't see any reason why your life should change.'

As he spoke his eyes assessed Davina thoughtfully, and suddenly she realised that while done with the best of intentions, the way her uncle had worded his will might have placed her in a very difficult position.

Chapter Two

'What the hell's that?' asked Phil, sitting up in bed and listening intently.

'I can't hear anything,' murmured Davina sleepily.

'It sounds as though we're living next to a motorway.'

She propped herself up on one elbow. 'Oh God, it must be the removal vans. Jay phoned and said they'd be arriving over the weekend. It's lucky I got the last of Uncle David's things out of the house yesterday.'

'You didn't tell me Jay Prescott had rung you.' Phil sounded accusing.

'It didn't seem important,' said Davina truthfully. 'Anyway, you were so late getting here last night we didn't have time to talk about anything much.'

'More to the point we didn't have time to *do* anything much,' he said, sliding a hand beneath the hem of Davina's night-dress. 'Now we're awake I think we ought to remedy that.'

Davina sighed inwardly. Since her uncle's death her sex life had taken a turn for the worse. Phil was less thoughtful, and although nothing had been said Davina sensed he was still annoyed that she hadn't inherited everything. It was as though he was blaming her, which was utterly ridiculous. It was also disconcerting to realise how much he'd counted on her owning the estate one day.

'I'm not sure I'm in the mood,' she murmured.

'Of course you are,' said Phil, his left hand gripping her right breast and giving her nipple a perfunctory tweak before he slid his body on top of hers. 'Couldn't you get a shorter night-dress?' he complained, as the material caught beneath him.

Davina struggled to remove it and by the time she'd thrown it to the floor Phil was inside her, pumping rhythmically, his hands heavy on her breasts. She noticed that he no longer bothered to kiss her when they were having sex; instead he gazed at the wall ahead of him, concentrating solely on his own pleasure.

Just as the first tiny flicker of arousal began deep within Davina, Phil shuddered and gasped then rolled off her. 'Did you manage to come too?' he asked.

Davina felt both used and angry. 'Of course I didn't. It takes me more than four-and-a-half minutes you know'

'I didn't realise I was being timed.' Phil sounded equally angry.

Suddenly Davina couldn't bear to stay in the bed with him a minute longer. 'I'm going to make some coffee,' she said as she got up.

'You've got a great figure,' said Phil appreciatively. 'I like girls with long, lean legs and high buttocks. I wouldn't mind your tits being a bit bigger, but otherwise I've no complaints.' He laughed.

'Perhaps you'd like me to have some plastic surgery?' suggested Davina.

'Hey, come on, I was only kidding,' said Phil.

'Unfortunately I don't feel quite as cheerful as you do,' she said.

Once in the kitchen, with her silk robe caressing her sensitive and unsatisfied flesh, Davina stared out of the window. Her eyes widened in surprise at the sight of six enormous removal vans parked in a row along the drive of the main house. She hoped there wouldn't be too many more or they'd have to queue up the road. Thankfully she didn't have to do anything to help Jay move in. He'd assured her that the removal men would see to everything, but she had to admit to herself that she was rather looking forward to his arrival on Monday. It would be interesting to see him again because she realised that, probably due to the circumstances of their meeting, she couldn't remember him very clearly. Not that she intended to share these feelings with Phil. The very mention of Jay Prescott's name was enough to put him in a bad mood and she wanted a peaceful weekend.

For the next two days the pair of them did all the things they usually did during Phil's visits; they went for walks, taking Major, David's Labrador, with them as the dog was living with Davina until she discovered what the American thought of animals. In the evenings they went out to eat at local pubs. It was nearly midnight on the Sunday before Phil left, and he was obviously reluctant to go.

'Are you going to be all right this week?'

'Why shouldn't I be?'

'You've got this American chap to handle. He's a prosecutor, hardly the kind of man you're used to dealing with.'

'Meaning what?'

'Meaning that he's probably got a mind as sharp as a razor and a tongue to match. I don't want you hurt by him, Davina.'

'Why should he hurt me?' she asked in astonishment. 'We hardly need to see each other once he's settled in.'

'I still don't like it, and I don't know what your uncle was thinking of when he drew up the will. It isn't right having you living here alone in the grounds with a man like that only a few hundred metres away.'

'You make him sound like a criminal,' laughed Davina. 'He looked to me like a man whose work is the most important thing in his life.'

'I don't see how you could possibly know that.'

Davina shrugged. 'It's that air of authority he had about him, and his businesslike behaviour. You have to admit he wasn't exactly a smooth charmer.'

'Maybe not, but you noticed what he was like all right, didn't you?'

'You're not jealous, are you?' she asked incredulously. Phil shook his head. 'Not of him being here with you, just of his inheriting the estate.'

Davina wanted to remind Phil that the estate was nothing to do with him, that the pair of them weren't even engaged and that if anyone felt upset about losing out on the inheritance it should be her, but as usual she kept quiet. 'Drive carefully and have a safe journey,' she said, kissing him on the cheek.

'That's not very passionate,' he complained.

As he grabbed her, crushing his lips against hers, Davina realised that she was simply waiting for him to go. When she heard his car drive away she let out a sigh of relief and her shoulders sagged as the tension drained out of them. There was no doubt about it, their relationship was falling apart, but whether it was Phil's fault or hers she wasn't sure.

Jay Prescott unfolded his long legs and slid out of the driving seat of the Aston Martin that a friend had managed to get for him from a second-hand car dealer. He'd always wanted to own an Aston Martin and had greatly enjoyed the drive from London. 'What do you think, Pattie?' he asked the leggy blonde climbing out of the passenger seat.

'I think it's great,' she enthused. 'I love speed.'

'I meant the house,' he said evenly. There were times when Pattie irritated him, but the sex between them was so incredible that he never let it show. They'd been together for six months and he still wasn't bored; quite a record for him. He suspected it was because she was wonderfully inventive and willing to indulge all his desires, which was more than some of his girlfriends had been.

Pattie smoothed down her dark blue lycra mini-skirt and tugged at the white silk halter-neck top, which emphasised her cosmetically-enhanced breasts. Although only twenty-eight she was very anxious to keep the ravages of time at bay, and being the ex-wife of a millionaire could well afford to do this. 'Kinda cute,' she said brightly.

'Cute? You're talking about a piece of English heritage. Dolls are cute, puppies are cute, old English houses are magnificent.'

'Okay,' she agreed amicably, 'it's magnificent. I just hope it's got central heating and a decent shower. You know what the Brits are like when it comes to central heating. They seem to imagine that there's something uplifting about freezing to death.'

'I don't imagine for one moment that this house has central heating,' retorted Jay. 'I don't think my god-father had the money to heat a place this size.'

'But you have, haven't you?' Pattie pointed out.

'Sure I have,' agreed Jay. 'But I don't know if I'm going to bother. It depends on how much time I spend here.'

'You're going to be here a year! Even you can't manipulate things so that that doesn't include a winter.'

'I guess not,' he agreed.

'Was your godfather married?'

Jay shook his head. 'He left a trail of broken hearts behind him in his youth and then settled down here on his own. He used to pop up to London now and again for discreet visits to lady friends but his work meant everything to him.'

'You must have been blood relations, he sounds just like you.'

Jay shook his head. 'Nope, but he and my father were good friends and we got on well. You're right though, in many ways we were alike. The last time he visited America he came and listened to me in court. He said some pretty kind things about me.'

'So does everyone,' said Pattie, walking up the steps and lifting the brass knocker. 'I only asked because I hoped he'd got a large bed.'

'Since we hardly ever use the bed for sex it doesn't really matter, does it?' Jay pointed out. 'We've got enough rooms here to keep us happy for six years. I'm going to ask Todd and Tanya over once we're settled in.'

Pattie's eyes gleamed. 'Fantastic! We can have a housewarming party, although perhaps it had better be called a housefreezing party.'

Jay glanced over his shoulder at the cottage they'd passed as they came through the gates. 'Ask Clive to take our cases in,' he said to Pattie. 'Then we ought to pay a visit on Davina.'

'Oh yeah, the niece. I bet she's ticked off.'

'Not inheriting the house you mean?'

Pattie nodded. 'Sure. I mean you said she claimed never to have heard of you. She must have imagined the whole lot was going to her.'

Jay considered this for a moment. 'She didn't strike me as that kind of girl,' he said at last.

'What's she like?' asked Pattie, wondering if this English niece was going to offer competition, because Pattie was prepared to fight tooth and nail in a no-holds-barred war to keep her away from Jay if necessary. Marriage to Jay would give her an excellent position in Bostonian society, a position that she would never be able to obtain any other way. Also, sex with him was incredible.

'She's a bit taller than you with short, dark, curly hair, slim and intelligent looking,' said Jay.

'Is she attractive?'

He shrugged. 'Yeah I guess, in a wholesome kinda way. She wears classy clothes.'

Pattie flushed. 'What do you mean by that?'

Jay smiled to himself. He'd known that would sting. Pattie had no idea of class; it was the one thing money hadn't been able to buy for her. Not that he objected, that wasn't why he was with her, but he was well aware that it was an area of vulnerability. He always liked to know people's weaknesses and anxieties as you never knew when they might prove useful.

An hour later he and Pattie arrived at the cottage. Davina answered the door to them wearing a pair of black velvet trousers and a red and grey dog-tooth jacket over a cream blouse. He'd been right, Jay thought to himself, she had class. On the other hand she didn't look as though she had very much experience and he wondered what she was like in bed.

He watched with interest as she ran a hand through her hair. 'You should have phoned me, told me you were coming,' she babbled. 'The place is an absolute tip. I've been working in the studio all day and ...'

'It's your cottage,' said Jay. 'Doesn't matter to me if it's a tip or not. As long as you service me when required, the place is your own.'

Colour stained her normally pale cheeks and he felt excitement stir within him. He'd been careful with his use of words, suspecting that she'd find them unsettling, and as he walked into the cottage he could tell that she was uneasy.

'Now this *is* cute,' enthused Pattie, who hadn't been listening to her lover. 'You say you've been working in your studio. Are you a ballet dancer?'

'Does she look as though she's been working out at the barre in those clothes?' asked Jay.

Now it was Pattie's turn to flush. 'I guess not. I wasn't thinking.'

'Obviously.'

'Is everything all right for you at the house?' asked Davina anxiously, moving restlessly around her living room. 'Clive said that the removal men were excellent and everything was in place.'

'It looks fine,' Jay reassured her. 'If you don't mind I'd like to have a look at your studio and the work you do there.' He was surprised when Davina seemed about to refuse. 'Do you have a problem with that?' he asked in his best prosecutor's manner.

'Not a problem exactly,' stammered Davina. 'It's just that some of the pictures I'm doing at the moment are a bit risqué.'

Pattie laughed, linking one arm in Jay's and running a hand over his chest and down to his waist, her long fingernails scratching lightly just above his belt.

'You don't need to worry about Jay, honey. He's very broad-minded.'

'Well, all right then,' Davina agreed reluctantly and, intrigued, Jay walked into the studio.

There were pictures everywhere, on the walls, on the

floor, stacked in the corners, and large sketches at various stages of development were on different drawing boards. As Davina stood uncomfortably in the middle of the room, her hands clasped tightly together, Jay prowled around, fascinated by the erotic drawings that were clearly her latest pieces.

'It seems you've got hidden depths,' he drawled.

He could tell she was embarrassed. 'I'm freelance, I have to take any work I can get,' she said defensively.

'Sure, but you couldn't do it if you didn't know about this kind of thing.'

'It's science-fiction, a fantasy,' explained Davina.

'In other words, you use your imagination, is that what you're saying?'

'Yes ... that is, no.'

'It must be one or the other.'

'Don't worry about him,' laughed Pattie. 'Jay doesn't have conversations, he conducts cross-examinations.'

She looked at the picture her lover was studying, wriggling between him and the drawing board and then pressing her buttocks back against him until Jay felt himself responding. As his erection stirred inside his trousers he put his arms around Pattie's waist and nuzzled the nape of her neck for a minute, while she continued to wriggle enthusiastically.

Jay was well aware that Davina was embarrassed by Pattie's behaviour and this amused him. He was so used to Pattie that normally he ignored her, but the drawings had aroused him as well. He supposed that if he analysed his reaction it wasn't so much the drawings as the fact that they'd been done by this cool, rather innocent-looking young woman standing defensively in her studio, obviously longing for the pair of them to leave. He remembered her boyfriend from the day of the funeral. He hadn't looked anything special. Jay couldn't imagine that Davina had drawn any ideas for the pictures from him.

Eventually, as Pattie continued to writhe, Jay realised that they were going to have to leave and continue things back at the house. He moved the blonde to one side and turned his attention to Davina. 'I just wanted to let you know that we were here. Perhaps you could stop by the house at ten tomorrow morning and I'll tell you about the first dinner party I'm arranging. I'll need your help with that.'

'Of course,' responded Davina.

'We can show ourselves out,' continued Jay, and he saw a look of relief cross the English girl's face. 'Why don't you get back to work?' he suggested.

'Now?'

'Sure, I'd like to see you working on that picture.'

'I can't work with other people around.'

'Well that's a pity, honey, because I want you to and as I understood it from the will, what I want has a distinct bearing on whether or not you remain in the cottage.'

'My work isn't a service for you,' protested Davina.

'I think it'll relax me to watch you at work. Are you refusing?'

He saw the indecision on her face as she tried to work out what she should do. Then, clearly deciding that she was in no position to argue at such an early stage in their relationship, she sat down on the high stool and began to draw. Jay moved nearer, standing directly behind her, and as he inhaled the light fragrance of her perfume he reached out and very lightly touched her on the shoulder. She jerked as though a bolt of electricity had shot through her and her pencil fell to the floor.

'Blast!' she muttered.

'You seem very nervous,' said Jay, turning away so that she couldn't see the amusement on his face. 'Maybe you'll feel more relaxed now that you know there's someone living in the main house again?'

'Maybe.' Her voice was low, and since he knew perfectly well that he was the one putting her on edge he knew that she was in a dilemma. She could hardly come out and say that she'd been perfectly relaxed until he arrived, even though it was evident that this was the truth.

'Come on, Jay,' Pattie urged, grabbing hold of his hand and kissing the side of his neck. 'We've got some important business back at the house.'

'Remember,' Jay called over his shoulder as he and Pattie left, 'I need to see you at the main house tomorrow at ten sharp.'

'I won't forget,' said Davina.

Jay knew that she wouldn't. In fact, she probably wouldn't be able to get the thought out of her head all night, and the realisation gave him immense pleasure. He enjoyed playing games with people. Manipulating Davina was going to be very interesting.

*

Pattie lay on the study floor, her mini-skirt hitched up round her waist, her silk hold-up stockings discarded and her long legs draped over Jay's shoulders as he knelt between her outstretched thighs.

She was trembling with excitement and could feel her juices as he opened her sex lips, ran his tongue up and down the tender flesh between them and then let them close again.

'For God's sake don't keep me waiting any longer,' she shouted, arching her hips up off the floor, but she knew it was pointless. One of the things that excited her about Jay was the fact that he was a control freak. He gave her fantastic pleasure but only when he wanted to, and that, together with the sexual games he and his friends played, had opened up a whole new world to her. Just the same, right at this moment, when all she wanted was to come, it could be frustrating.

She felt him open her up slowly once more and again his tongue glided across her damp flesh. The tip flicked inside her entrance, circling round the sensitive nerve endings, and a searing flash of pleasure streaked through her so that she felt certain she was about to come. Then, as though sensing this, Jay once more lifted his head and allowed her sex lips to close, massaging them briefly with the heel of his hand until the whole area felt swollen and hot and tingles of pleasure suffused her.

She was so near to coming that she whimpered in disbelief when he moved until he was lying beside her and turned his attention to her breasts, instead of the throbbing, aching area between her thighs that craved his touch so desperately. 'Enjoying yourself?' he asked casually, the fingers of his right hand gripping the tip of one nipple with increasing pressure until she felt it start to throb with discomfort, a discomfort that would eventually turn to a dark pleasure that was sometimes enough to trigger an orgasm on its own.

'I want to come!' she screamed at him. 'Stop playing games with me.'

'I enjoy watching you like this,' he said calmly. 'You look wonderful, so dishevelled and wanton.'

Pattie didn't want to see herself. All she wanted was for her body to be racked by an intense climax, a climax that she'd been keenly anticipating from the moment she'd started arousing Jay back at the cottage. 'What do you want me to do?' she asked.

'Just be patient.'

'I don't feel patient, godammit.'

He gave one of his rare smiles. 'I know you don't, that's half the fun of all this.' Suddenly his fingers pinched her nipple hard and she squealed, a squeal that quickly changed to a moan as the delicious, dangerous excitement coursed through her body and she felt her stomach muscles start to ripple. 'I'm gonna come,' she warned him.

'I guess I've kept you waiting long enough,' he admitted regretfully. Once more he knelt between her thighs, her legs raised in the air. This time when he parted her sex lips, he fastened his mouth over her swollen, aching clitoris and began to suck at it rhythmically. Pattie moaned with delight and when he thrust two fingers inside her, pressing upwards against her G-spot while at the same time continuing to suck on the bunched nerve endings that were the centre of all her pleasure, her frantic body finally succumbed and her climax crashed over her in glorious hot pulsating waves.

When the last tiny contractions had died away Jay pulled her to her feet, stood behind her and bent her forward so that her long blonde hair was hanging down, almost brushing the tops of her feet. Knowing what was going to happen next she parted her legs and braced herself as he thrust inside her, driving in and out in a steady rhythm while at the same time his hands squeezed her full, perfectly formed breasts until, silently as usual, he came, his hips shuddering as his body slammed against hers in a final passionate frenzy.

Pattie felt him withdraw the moment his climax was over, and not just physically but emotionally. She thought how strange it was that a man capable of giving a woman such intense physical pleasure should be so disinterested in emotional contact.

'There, now we've christened the new house,' he remarked, readjusting his clothing.

'Why did you make me wait so long?' she asked.

He looked surprised at the question. 'Because I enjoy it. In any case, you have better climaxes when you're made to wait for them, or hadn't you noticed?'

'Of course I'd noticed,' said Pattie. 'But I wasn't sure that was the reason.'

'You should never try to analyse sex,' remarked Jay. 'It's a big mistake. Either it works or it doesn't.'

'Luckily for me it always works with you,' said Pattie, putting her arms round him. He stood passively for a moment but then she felt him stiffen and knew that she had to let him go. He wasn't keen on physical contact except during sex. Early on in their relationship she, being a tactile young woman, had frequently taken his hand or hugged him, but he'd quickly put her straight in that regard. Now she knew better. It was just that sometimes, particularly when they'd had good sex, she'd have liked to feel his arms around her.

'Something wrong?' asked Jay.

Silently Pattie cursed herself. Jay never missed a thing, probably because of his profession. He even seemed to be able to read her thoughts. 'Of course not.'

'Fine. If you were discontented I hope you'd let me know.'

'Discontented? How could I ever be discontented with you?'

'Plenty of other women have been,' he said calmly. 'Now, it's time I looked round the place with Clive, not just the house but the estate as well.'

'I guess I'll take a shower and freshen up,' said Pattie.

'It was quite a surprise seeing that girl's work at the cottage, wasn't it?'

Jay, who had reached the doorway, turned his head sharply. 'A surprise?'

'Why do you always answer questions with questions?' asked Pattie.

'Do I?'

She laughed. 'There you go again. It only surprised me because she didn't seem that sort of a person.'

'If there's one thing I've learnt in my line of work it's that people's outward appearances are very deceptive,' said Jay. 'Except in your case,' he added. 'You're pretty much like I expected.'

'Good,' said Pattie, but when Jay had left the room she frowned, uncertain that his words were a compliment.

Alone in the cottage after her visitors had gone, Davina found it impossible to settle back to work. Jay's presence had affected her in an extraordinary way. She'd been incredibly aware of him; aware of the way his long-fingered hands had reached out and touched her work, of his short brown hair lying flat and neat against his head and above all of his breath against the nape of her neck when he'd stood behind her while she was working. She'd felt gauche, and worst of all childish in his presence, although nothing he'd said or done had indicated that he found her so. It was simply that he made her feel small. She supposed it had something to do with his size, but it was much more than that as well. 'Pull yourself together,' she said sharply, as she found herself wondering what he and his blonde companion were doing back at the house. 'He's nothing to you except your landlord.' But even that didn't quieten her racing brain because it reminded her of the way the will had been worded, and his own words when he'd visited. She was certain that he intended to use the clause in the will for procuring some kind of sexual favour, yet she couldn't really believe that a man like that would be so desperate for female attention. Perhaps, she thought with horror, it was what she wanted rather than what he wanted. The thought was shaming.

Eventually she took a shower, deciding that this might calm her, but when the needles of warm water hit her flesh she started to feel aroused and to her astonishment her breasts began to swell, the nipples standing erect, so that without thinking she ran her hands over the small globes. She caressed them softly, lathering them and spreading the bubbles over each nipple in a tender caress that did far more for her than anything Phil had done lately.

She was more aroused now than she'd been for several months and her right hand slid over her belly, working its way between her dark pubic hair until she could lightly stroke her slowly swelling clitoris. She could hear her own breathing, quick and shallow, and her legs were starting to tremble as her whole body tightened. Reaching up Davina unhooked the shower head, leant back against the wall of the cubicle, her feet either side of the mat and thrust her hips forward so that the spray of water fell directly onto her pubic mound.

Almost at once delicious sensations curled upwards, travelling through her belly to her breasts, and as her right hand played the water over her vulva she used her left hand to continue stroking her breasts, her eyes half closed and her lips slightly parted with the sheer hedonistic pleasure of it all.

She'd never done anything like this in her life before

but as her need for a climax grew she reluctantly released her tight little nipple and used her left hand to open herself up as fully as possible. As soon as the stinging spray from the shower touched the stimulated nerve endings her pleasure spilt and she felt the glorious hot, liquid warmth spreading through her while her entire body shook violently.

When it was over she replaced the shower head, turned off the water and stepped quickly out of the cubicle, wrapping herself in a large fluffy towel that she'd placed over the heated rail. Already surprised by her own sensuality she was startled to find that even the touch of the soft fabric against her skin was pleasurable, and as she dried herself her nipples hardened again. She knew why, but she didn't want to admit it. The truth was that all the time she'd been masturbating, and even now while she was drying herself, she was imagining Jay Prescott, his lean hard body entwined around his beautiful leggy blonde mistress. It was this that had really excited her.

Once dressed Davina found that she was hungry and then, having eaten, realised that she wanted to work again. Without pausing to analyse why, she hurried into the studio and within minutes was sitting on the stool, her pencil flying busily over the paper. She didn't stop for nearly half an hour and then it was only the ache in her neck that made her straighten up. When she glanced at her work she was stunned. She didn't know how she'd done it but the picture was full of the most incredible erotic passion.

The expression on the woman's face was different from any expression Davina had ever drawn before: sensual, arousing and sated all at the same time, while the man had an air of command about him that had been lacking earlier. His possession of the woman was obviously total, his domination over her absolute and this, Davina realised, was exactly how it was meant to be.

As she turned out the lamp Davina knew, without a shadow of doubt, that this was the best work she'd ever done. 'Thank you, Jay,' she murmured, then shivered. If he could have that much of an effect on her work, what kind of an effect would he have on her life?

Chapter Three

When Davina arrived for their meeting the next morning Jay was already waiting for her outside the front door and glanced pointedly at his watch. 'You're late.'

'Surely not.'

'I thought we agreed ten o'clock.'

Davina glanced at her watch. 'What time is it then?'

'Four minutes past.'

For a moment she thought he was teasing her, but quickly realised her mistake. Perhaps time mattered more in American courts, she thought. 'Next time I'll run,' she told him.

'It would be easier if you left on time. I thought we'd have coffee on the lawn as it's such a lovely morning. Clive will bring it out to us.'

Sitting down on one of two loungers clearly placed there earlier for their benefit, Davina noticed how smart Jay looked. He was wearing a brown and green sports jacket over a white open-necked shirt and his slacks were a pale fawn, immaculately pressed. All at once she was uncomfortably aware of the fact that her jeans had paint on them, and there was a small tear in the sleeve of her cotton top.

'I thought I'd like to kick off with a dinner party on Saturday night for six people,' he explained. 'A couple of friends of mine are flying in from the States on Friday, Todd Lattimer and his wife Tanya. They're a nice couple; she's his third wife and it seems like he's finally found the right woman. They'll be staying here for a few weeks. Todd's a deputy District Attorney and my immediate boss. He's quite an Anglophile and should love this place. It would be nice if you could organise a meal that he'll remember.'

'That won't be a problem,' Davina assured him. 'Do he and his wife have any particular likes or dis-likes?'

Jay's hazel eyes were thoughtful. 'Of course they do. What area of their lives are you referring to?'

Davina felt thoroughly irritated. 'Are you always this pedantic?'

'In my job every word counts. You have to say what you mean.'

'But from what I hear you don't necessarily have to mean what you say, at least not in court.'

'Are you referring to American courts or your own justice system?' he asked, seeming intrigued.

'I don't suppose our systems are that different,' she said hastily, realising that she couldn't afford to antagonise him. 'In any case, I was referring to food.'

'I think they eat anything.'

'Who are the other two guests?'

'Why, yourself and your boyfriend of course. I thought I'd already made that clear.'

Davina shook her head. 'You never mentioned it.'

'How stupid of me. Well, I've mentioned it now. Since you've lived here for some time you'll be better placed than I am to answer any questions Todd may have about the area.' Davina, who'd half hoped he'd asked her because he thought she'd be good company, felt irrationally disappointed at his explanation. It seemed so impersonal, but then that was his style.

After Clive had placed coffee and biscuits on the small table in front of them and returned to the house, Jay lifted his face towards the sun and gave a small sigh. 'Someone told me your climate was dreadful but this is very agreeable.'

'The trouble is we don't get many days like this,' explained Davina. 'What's it like in Boston?'

'It could be raining for all I know. I haven't spoken to anyone there today.'

'I meant in general,' she said crossly.

'Right, in general. In general the summers are quite good and the winters very cold but there's a lot of rain. There, has that satisfied your very English desire for a discussion on weather?'

'Yes thank you,' said Davina shortly.

'Excellent, then perhaps we can progress to the menu. Have you given it any thought?'

Davina felt very pleased with herself. 'Yes I have. I thought it would be nice if we began with a warm mushroom salad, followed by beef cooked with black olives and English vegetables, then for dessert a passion fruit and mango mousse.'

'Sounds great,' agreed Jay. 'Well balanced and nice

and English. Incidentally, I like people to dress up at dinner. I'm not in favour of this new uniform of jeans and T-shirt that seems to be worn everywhere.' He looked pointedly at her outfit.

'Neither am I,' said Davina. 'These are my working clothes. I'm repainting the kitchen at the moment, in between doing my drawings. I promise I won't turn up at your dinner party wearing jeans.'

'Good, because I like a woman to look like a woman. I'm not very politically correct. I believe there are basic differences between the sexes which means they can never be truly equal.'

'That sounds like an interesting topic for discussion on Saturday,' said Davina, refusing to rise to the bait as he watched her with a gleam of anticipation in his eyes. 'Thanks very much for the coffee, it was delicious. Are you likely to have any typing for me?' she added.

Jay frowned. 'Typing?'

'I used to type for my uncle. Since you're in the legal profession I thought there might be case studies and things that you needed typed up.'

'I couldn't possibly hand my work out to anyone but a legal secretary. I do have my reputation to consider.'

'Fine, but I didn't want you to think I wasn't willing to work for my cottage.'

Jay moved his left hand slowly over the table until his fingers were resting on the top of Davina's hand. 'Don't worry, Davina, there are plenty of things that you'll be able to do for me. Believe me, you'll earn your cottage.'

She felt herself start to tremble and snatched her hand away. 'Fine, I've always liked to be independent.'

Jay rose to his feet. 'I assume you're used to dropping in at the main house whenever you feel like it. Now that I'm here perhaps you'd be good enough to ring through before you leave the cottage. Sometimes I might be busy, or it may simply be inconvenient to have you call.' He looked across the garden and Davina saw Pattie walking towards them. 'I'm sure you get my drift,' he added.

Davina's face felt hot. 'I certainly do.' Suddenly she couldn't wait to be gone, to get away from this difficult, detached stranger who was having the most peculiar effect on her.

'Hi,' said Pattie, greeting Davina with a wide smile that showed off her perfect set of even white teeth to great advantage. 'I've been looking round the grounds here, you've got a cute little summerhouse.'

'It's a gazebo,' said Davina.

Pattie looked surprised. 'What's the difference?'

'Look it up in a dictionary,' said Jay. 'I'm always telling you that's the best way to improve your mind.'

Pattie laughed. 'It isn't my mind that interests him,' she told Davina, and wrapped herself around her lover, kissing him passionately. Jay didn't move. He neither encouraged her nor attempted to push her off, instead he stood there passively, but his eyes were watching Davina. Suddenly, without knowing why, she couldn't bear to watch any more and turning away she hurried back to the solitude of her cottage, which for some reason didn't seem quite as welcoming as usual.

'Where did you get that?' asked Phil as Davina stood in front of the bedroom mirror adjusting her oyster-coloured satin two-piece. 'I've never seen it before.'

'I bought it in Oxford this week,' she explained.

'It looks expensive.'

'It didn't cost you anything.'

He frowned. 'That's not what I meant. What's so

special about tonight that you felt you had to go out and buy yourself a fancy outfit?'

The truth was Davina didn't know why she'd done it. Phil was quite right; the outfit had been outrageously expensive, but with its long elegant skirt and beautifully cut tunic that reached just below her hips and was embroidered with large swirls, it made her look and feel both elegant and sexy. She'd needed it in order to feel confident enough to face Jay and his friends, particularly after learning that his boss was to be there. All that she knew about American lawyers had been gleaned from watching videos and TV movies, but she was very aware that they were rich. She wanted to show that she wasn't some poor relation living off charity.

'You haven't answered me,' persisted Phil.

'It was an impulse buy.'

'I'm not looking forward to the evening at all.' Phil's expression was truculent. 'It's not as though I know any of these people.'

'Neither do I,' said Davina. 'At least, only Pattie.'

'Then why are we going?'

'Because Jay thought that his boss would like to meet

some English people,' she explained, consoling herself with the thought that this wasn't entirely a lie even though Jay hadn't mentioned Phil by name.

'I can't stand the man,' continued Phil moodily. 'He's the sort of American that gives the country a bad name.'

'I didn't know it had a bad name,' laughed Davina. 'Besides, you only dislike him because he inherited the house. He's probably a very nice person underneath.'

'Underneath what?'

'Underneath that veneer of being a not very nice person! Come on, Phil. Don't be cross. Let's try and enjoy ourselves. At least you know the food will be good.' She stood in front of him and gave a twirl. 'What do you think?'

'Like I said, expensive.'

This time Davina's sigh was audible. 'I do hope you're not going to sulk the whole evening. If you think about it, it was nice of Jay to invite us.'

'Is that how you see it? In my opinion he's damn lucky to be living there. You should be the one throwing a dinner party for *my* boss.'

'Even if I had inherited the house I don't see why I

would have felt it necessary to entertain your boss,' replied Davina. 'Come on, we mustn't be late. He's a stickler for punctuality.'

'That figures,' muttered Phil.

When they arrived at the house everyone was gathered in the drawing room for drinks and it was there that Davina had her first glimpse of Todd and Tanya Lattimer. Todd looked to be in his mid-forties, his thick hair was completely silver but it was obvious that he kept himself in good physical shape, and his blue eyes sparkled as he took Davina's hand and kissed her on the cheek. 'Delighted to meet you, Davina. Jay's told us all about your uncle's death. Please accept our condolences.'

Davina felt an unexpected lump in her throat. 'That's very kind of you,' she whispered. 'I'm afraid I still miss him dreadfully.'

'Sure you do. No one would expect anything different. I'd like you to meet my wife, Tanya. Tanya, this is Davina Fletcher, Jay's godfather's niece.'

Tanya Lattimer was quite a surprise to Davina. She was of medium height and slender build. It was obvious from her straight, jet-black hair, cut stylishly short and her slightly slanted dark eyes that there was Oriental blood in her. Dressed in a flowing ankle-length sleeveless over-dress and a pair of lime green silk trousers which toned in with the lime and turquoise top, she looked extraordinarily striking. It was clear from the way she looked at her husband that she was deeply in love with him.

'You're just as Jay described you,' she said with a smile.

'I don't know whether that's a compliment or not,' laughed Davina.

Todd nodded enthusiastically. 'Oh yeah, it's a compliment all right.'

'Time to go in to dinner,' said Jay, coming up to their group. He nodded at Davina but, much to her disappointment, didn't attempt to take her hand or kiss her. 'Glad you were on time.'

Todd laughed. 'I take it you've already discovered young Jay's penchant for rules and regulations.'

'Be careful, darling,' said Tanya, slipping her hand into Todd's. 'You mustn't give away Jay's secrets.'

'Oh, don't worry,' said Davina hastily. 'I know he likes things to happen at precisely the time he's arranged.'

'That's not exactly what I meant,' said Tanya, then turned and left the room, leaving Davina to wonder what she was trying to infer.

The dinner went well and Davina was delighted with the way all the guests tucked into the food. Pattie, wearing an ankle-length sleeveless black dress with white bands around the armhole, neckline and just beneath her ample breasts, that fitted her like a second skin, even asked Davina for the recipe for the beef.

'Why do you want to know that?' enquired Jay curiously. 'You can't even boil an egg.'

'I thought I might learn to become domesticated while we're here,' said Pattie. 'Either that or take up gardening.'

'She's kidding,' said Todd to Davina, who was sitting on his right. 'The most energetic thing Pattie does is get out of bed in the morning.'

'I do an aerobic workout every day,' said Pattie indignantly. 'How else do you think I keep my figure?'

'By regular visits to your plastic surgeon,' drawled Jay.

'Of course,' said Phil. 'I'd forgotten that you come from the land of the knife.'

Jay stiffened slightly but his expression remained neutral. 'Meaning what?'

'Meaning that you Americans believe the knife is the answer to everything, don't you? Not just knives either. You use knives to slice and dice and keep yourselves forever young, and guns to shoot each other when you want a change of partner.'

'That's a helluva sweeping statement,' said Jay calmly. 'Perhaps you'd like to justify it.'

'I don't see why I need to,' snapped Phil. 'We're forever reading in the papers about tourists getting shot at in Florida. Seems a strange place to have Disney World when you think about it. Doesn't the tourist board have a list of recommendations about never moving out of your designated hotel area and—'

'You don't have any crime here I take it?' said Jay.

'Sure we have crime, but we also have strict gun laws. Mind you, it seems to me that the American male lacks self-confidence. His gun seems to reinforce his manhood.'

'Is that a fact?'

'You must see it in court all the time,' said Phil, his mouth set in a firm line.

'I see all kinds of things in the courtroom,' said Jay. 'Sure there are murders, but you have murders here, and gross miscarriages of justice as well . . .'

'Such as?'

'Derek Bentley.' There was an awkward silence.

'Okay, so that was a mistake,' agreed Phil. 'But at least we no longer execute killers. If the Derek Bentley case happened today it would all be very different.'

'But it didn't happen today, did it? The fact that you don't execute killers any more isn't of any help to Derek Bentley. In any case, as I understand it the average British citizen would like to see capital punishment brought back. Fair to say?'

'I've no idea,' said Phil.

'Oh come on, Phil,' exclaimed Davina. 'You know Jay's telling the truth. If you held a national referendum next week the majority of people would vote for bringing back capital punishment.'

'Only for certain crimes,' protested Phil.

'Ah I see,' said Jay. 'So it'll be okay to hang the wrong person for, say, killing a child or a policeman, will it?'

'No.'

'But if you introduce that kind of system there's bound to be mistakes.'

'I didn't say I wanted that system brought in,' protested Phil.

'But you agree that most of your countrymen do?'

Phil's cheeks were flushed. 'Let's just forget it, shall we?'

'I was enjoying myself,' said Jay, and Davina could tell from the brightness of his eyes that he was telling the truth. Unfortunately, the same wasn't true of Phil and she decided that it was up to her to change the subject.

'I understand you like England,' she said to Todd, and for the next twenty minutes he and she talked together about the differences between their cultures. Phil, having decided he didn't wish to tangle with Jay again, became immersed in conversation with Pattie.

After dinner they moved into the large drawing room and Davina was astonished at the changes that had already been made to the house. The room looked fresh and clean, but at the same time Jay had retained its character. 'Do you approve?' he asked suddenly, coming up behind her so quietly that she wasn't aware of him.

Davina jumped. 'Yes, very much.'

'Good. You know, I do realise that I must have come as rather a nasty shock to you. Believe me, I had no idea your uncle was going to leave me this place, and while I don't suppose for one moment it means as much to me as it does to you I really value it. Despite what your boyfriend may think, not all Americans are completely vulgar. I feel it's a privilege that I've got the money to make the place look as good as it can. Maybe that's why your uncle left it to me rather than you.'

'It really doesn't matter,' Davina assured him. 'I've never thought about living here, and that's the truth.'

'Is it? I don't think your boyfriend feels like that.'

'I don't think it matters what Phil feels.'

'That's interesting,' Jay murmured, and he rested his right hand lightly on her shoulder. 'I thought the pair of you were a big item.'

Davina wished that he didn't have such an extraordinary effect on her. It was difficult to stop herself from shaking. Simply by touching her in a casual manner he created more desire in her than Phil created at the height of their lovemaking. 'We used to be, but I'm beginning to think I really don't know him very well.'

'Hardly surprising. I don't think any of us can expect to know another person very well. It's hard enough understanding ourselves.'

'But it's nice to be close to someone,' said Davina.

All at once Jay looked bored. 'Is that a fact? There, Davina, we'll have to agree to differ.' And with that he moved off.

At about two in the morning the dinner party broke up. As Phil went to fetch Davina's wrap she tried to find Jay to thank him for his hospitality. Todd and Tanya were in the dining room, Tanya perched on Todd's knee while he moved one hand rhythmically beneath her skirt.

There was no sign of their host, but just as she decided to leave anyway she heard the sound of Jay's voice from behind the slightly open door of the billiard room. Pushing on it she took a step into the room and then stopped in shock and embarrassment. Pattie was lying flat on her back on the billiard table, facing away from the door with her legs dangling over the edge, while Jay was kneeling on the floor with his head buried between her thighs. Pattie was gasping and moaning urgently, her hands reaching down and clutching spasmodically at Jay's hair, as she continued to whimper with increasing desire.

Rooted to the spot by the scene, Davina watched as Jay's hands slid up his girlfriend's body and began to lightly tease at her straining breasts, confined by her dress. The pair were so lost in the passion of the moment that neither of them was aware that they were being watched. As Davina attempted to creep away, she realised that Phil was standing behind her, his eyes wide, and she had to push him hard in the chest to get him to move.

'Time for us to go,' she hissed.

Phil peered over her shoulder. 'Fantastic tits,' he muttered.

'Yes, courtesy of one of the knives you were on about during dinner,' said Davina sharply, feeling a ridiculous surge of envy.

Phil frowned drunkenly. 'Was I? I can't remember,' he admitted.

'I'm not surprised with all the brandy you've drunk. Come on, we're going.' With that Davina walked swiftly out of the front door.

Once they were back in the bedroom of the cottage

Phil started fumbling amorously at her almost before she'd removed her outfit. Davina was so turned on by the startling image of Jay and Pattie in the billiard room that for once she was as keen as Phil.

'Let's do something different,' she whispered huskily. 'If you sit on the chair in front of the dressing table I'll sit on your lap.' As she spoke she suddenly remembered Tanya sitting on Todd's lap, and the way her husband's hand had been moving between her thighs.

'On a chair?' mumbled Phil. 'No thanks. The bed's good enough for me.'

'But it would be exciting,' persisted Davina.

'Stop talking, let's just do it,' he said, reaching out and pulling her down onto the bed with him. All at once Davina knew that she needed more than their usual predictable coupling. She pushed at Phil's shoulders, trying to get him to move his head between her thighs. To her disappointment he completely ignored her and simply licked and nibbled at her breasts for a few minutes, before rolling her onto her back, spreading her thighs and entering her. She was very wet, aroused by what she'd seen earlier, but Phil was so quick that despite this she wasn't able to reach a climax. In the early hours of the morning, as he lay deep in sleep beside her, she knew that her uncle had been right. She had never known passion. The problem was, who was going to teach her about it?

'Yes! Oh yes!' screamed Pattie, crouching on all fours on the billiard room floor while Jay thrust into her from behind. His hands were caressing her breasts, buttocks and clitoris, and his hips moved vigorously as he pounded into her after over an hour's foreplay.

Seated in the huge armchair, his wife sitting naked astride his massive erection, Todd Lattimer watched the other couple. As usual Pattie's excitement increased the sexual tension for him and Tanya.

Tanya was breathing rapidly as she lifted herself up and down, her hands resting on her husband's shoulders and her body angled forward so that with every thrust her G-spot was stimulated. Todd's eyes narrowed and he concentrated hard on his wife, anxious that his own pleasure shouldn't explode before she was fully satisfied. Out of the corner of his eye he saw Jay standing upright while Pattie lay in an exhausted heap on the floor.

'Would you like Jay to touch you?' he asked Tanya. She nodded and Jay padded across the room, reaching round the slender Oriental girl's body until his hands were gripping her almost boyish breasts fiercely.

Immediately the pupils of Tanya's eyes expanded and her lips parted as she began to groan with the delicious pleasure of it all. Jay crouched down and with delicate precision ran the tip of his tongue along Tanya's spine, lingering over every vertebrae and causing her body to tremble so violently that Todd felt his thighs shake beneath her.

'Are you nearly there?' he asked gently.

Tanya nodded and, managing to catch Jay's eye, Todd nodded slightly. Immediately Jay's hands increased the pressure on the imprisoned breasts, his fingers almost bruising the tender flesh. The result was electric. With a scream of ecstasy Tanya rode her husband's rigid cock ferociously, milking him with her internal muscles as her climax tore through her. Todd watched with delight as tiny beads of perspiration broke out on her top lip and the flush of arousal turned her upper chest and throat a deep pink.

'I'm going to come now,' he said huskily, and as Jay

walked away Todd finally spilled himself into his wife, unable to suppress a groan of ecstatic pleasure.

'I wonder what your tenant would have made of that?' she asked Jay when the four of them were dressing.

Jay looked thoughtful. 'She'd have been very shocked, and yet ...'

'Yet what?' asked Todd, intrigued.

'I get this feeling that there's a lot more to her than meets the eye.'

'You mean you want to involve her in our games?' asked Todd.

Jay shrugged. 'It might be amusing.'

'I'm not sure she's the kind of girl you should use simply as amusement,' replied his boss.

'What's the matter? It's not like you to pass up the chance of more fun.'

'Agreed, but is she sophisticated enough to be able to take care of herself?' queried Todd.

Jay hesitated for a moment. 'I reckon if I lead her to it gently, a step at a time, she could surprise you.'

'I like surprises,' laughed Todd.

'We all like surprises,' cried Pattie, finally summoning up the energy to get to her feet. 'You really reckon Davina would enjoy group sex, Jay?'

'Not if I walked up to her and said "Davina, would you like to come and join in an orgy at the main house next Saturday?".'

Pattie giggled. 'So how are you going to ask her?'

'I'm not going to ask her,' he said slowly. 'I'm simply going to encourage her, make her aware that there's more to life than that boring estate agent has shown her.'

'Why are you bothering?' asked Tanya.

'It's a challenge,' said Jay.

'Is that all?' asked Todd.

'Of course that's all. Besides, I've got an easy way of getting her started. Remember, she has to carry out any services I ask of her in order to keep her cottage.'

Tanya raised her eyebrows. 'I don't think joining in a group orgy was quite the kind of service her uncle had in mind when he wrote his will.'

'Maybe not, but I do know he wanted her horizons expanded and I think I'm the guy to do it.'

'Not on your own,' protested Pattie sharply. 'We'll all be involved.'

'Sure,' agreed Jay, then took her off to bed.

Todd and his wife remained sitting in the armchair, their bodies closely entwined. 'You know,' remarked Todd, 'I think Jay's fascinated by Davina. She's the right sort of woman for him too.'

Tanya nuzzled her husband's neck. 'Jay doesn't want a serious relationship, you know that, Todd. He just likes new experiences and he thinks Davina will offer him one.'

'Maybe, but I've got a hunch it could be more than that.'

'I hope you're right,' replied his wife. 'I'd like to see Jay become really involved with something other than his work.'

'I guess,' murmured her husband. 'But being single-minded has turned him into one helluva prosecutor.'

'One helluva lover too,' sighed Tanya. 'Davina may not know it yet, but she could be in for a very rewarding few months.'

Chapter Four

On the Monday following the dinner party, Davina was just about to go into her studio to start work when she glanced out of the window of her small front room and saw Jay Prescott walking towards the cottage. Her heart started to race as images of him and Pattie coupling furiously on the billiard table flashed through her brain. When he tapped on the front door she was reluctant to open it, shaken by his ability to affect her.

'Hi, hope I'm not interrupting your work,' he remarked, walking uninvited through the front door.

'I was just about to begin,' said Davina, startled by his arrogance.

'Lucky I came now. I don't imagine you'd have appreciated being interrupted.'

Remembering that he was the real owner of the cottage and that she was simply the tenant, Davina felt duty bound to offer some kind of hospitality. 'Would you like a coffee?'

Jay shook his head. 'I've come for the rent.'

Davina looked at him blankly. 'I thought you didn't have any typing for me?'

'Who said anything about typing?'

She frowned. 'What is it that you want me to do?'

'I'll explain in a minute. First, I'd like to thank you for Saturday night. The dinner was a great success. I hope you and Phil enjoyed yourselves?'

'I certainly did, but I'm not so sure about Phil.'

'I guess he's the kind of guy who can't bear to lose an argument.'

'Perhaps, but I suspect that you've never lost one yourself so you don't know what it feels like,' retorted Davina.

'You flatter me. I don't win all my cases you know. Some bad guys do get away.'

'And doubtless some good guys go down,' remarked Davina.

He nodded. 'Maybe, but they can always appeal. That's not my worry. I'm given a job to do and I do it. Which reminds me, my boss, Todd, thought the meal was fantastic. You certainly managed to impress him.'

'That was the object of the exercise, wasn't it?'

'Sure. Now, about other services that I require from you.'

'Yes?'

'I've brought a few things over with me. I want you to put them on and then start your work. I'll watch you for half an hour, then I'll go.'

Davina couldn't believe her ears. 'You've brought me clothes to wear while I work so that you can sit and watch me in them? What are you, some kind of pervert?'

'You haven't seen the clothes yet. Don't worry, it isn't a French maid's outfit.'

'I can't do it,' said Davina, feeling her heart thump against her ribs. 'I'm not some kind of whore.'

'What a terrible fuss you're making about a simple request. Why don't you look at the clothes before you take the moral high ground?'

Davina opened the box that he handed her. She took

out a peach-coloured silk blouse cut like a man's shirt, cream lace-trimmed French panties, a cream see-through camisole top, a pair of patterned cream hold-up stockings and a long strand of graduated pearls. The necklace had a matching pair of drop pearl earrings. Finally, at the bottom of the box, she found a pair of high-heeled cream shoes.

She didn't know what to say. Jay was standing on the far side of the room watching her with interest, and she suspected that he hoped she'd refuse so that he could be rid of her. On the other hand, it was clear that he was taking pleasure from the games that her uncle's will was allowing him to play. She felt that they were cat and mouse and she was the mouse.

As she stood uncertainly in the middle of the room her fingers instinctively caressed the blouse, and the feel of the expensive silk against her skin was wonderfully luxurious. Despite this she was still determined to refuse his request, until with a shock, she realised that she was damp between her thighs. The prospect of doing what he wanted was exciting her.

Now she didn't feel that he was using her. If she was going to get pleasure from it as well then how could it harm her, and it was pointless to deny the fact that she was attracted to Jay. She didn't believe for one moment that he was attracted to her, he was simply enjoying his power over her. At the same time, he was allowing her to experience sexual excitement and a desire for passion such as she'd never known before.

'All right,' she murmured, but she was unable to look at him as she spoke. 'I take it I am allowed to go up to my room to change?'

'Sure,' he said agreeably. 'I'll be waiting in your studio.'

Once she'd put the outfit on Davina looked at herself in the mirror and could hardly believe her eyes. Her long legs, emphasised by the high heels and the fact that the silk shirt only reached the top of her thighs, looked sexier than she'd ever seen them. The pearls, nestling coolly between the rounded tops of her breasts, made the overall effect far classier than it would otherwise have been. It was obvious that Jay had thought very carefully about the clothes.

It was only when she stood in the doorway of the studio and saw him waiting for her that Davina nearly lost her nerve. Her knees felt weak, but she forced herself to stand erect and hold her head high as she crossed the floor. She slid onto the high stool, which felt cold against the area of bare flesh between her panties and stocking tops.

'What do I do now?' she asked, irritated at the slight quaver in her voice.

Jay gestured towards the pencils on her desk. 'Start drawing,' he suggested. 'I take it that's what you normally do.'

With trembling fingers Davina grasped a pencil, bent over the drawing board and started work. She was incredibly aware of herself, of her whole body, and as she moved so the pearls moved, caressing her skin. All the time Jay prowled around the room, sometimes standing very close behind her and sometimes standing opposite her, giving himself, she realised, an excellent view of her cleavage.

Eventually it was time to add some colour to the drawing and she turned her upper body to reach for the paints. 'What are you doing?' he asked. When Davina explained Jay said, 'I don't want you getting paint on that lovely shirt. I think it's time you took it off.'

Now Davina started to tremble in earnest. The camisole top was sheer, and Jay would be able to see everything through it, including her shamefully hard nipples. She wished that he'd touch her. Her breasts were aching for the feel of his hands on them while her whole body seemed to have shed a layer of skin, leaving it unbelievably sensitive. Her breathing was quicker than normal and there was an ache between her thighs which made her shift uncomfortably on the stool.

After a short pause she obeyed, hoping that Jay would help her off with the shirt. He remained at a distance, however, and she had to get off the stool, walk in front of him and place it over the arm of a chair before returning to the drawing board. He said nothing, paid her no compliments and made no sound, but she knew that he was totally focused on her, that he wasn't missing a single movement she made. As time passed she crossed her legs, moving her right leg up and down her left and hearing the soft rubbing sound of silk against silk.

At this Jay appeared to stand even straighter. Glancing beneath lowered lids Davina saw that his hands were clenched so that his knuckles gleamed whitely. Surely now he'd do something, she thought to herself, almost mad with longing, and at precisely that moment he took a step towards her.

Davina looked up, feeling the blood rush to her cheeks as she stared at him, hoping that her eyes didn't betray her need. For a few seconds their eyes locked, then he glanced at his watch and turned away. 'Time for me to go.'

'Go?' she said stupidly.

'Yeah, you wore the clothes and I watched you in them. That's what I wanted, remember? That's your rent paid for another few days.'

Ridiculously she felt as though he'd rejected her, as though in some way she hadn't lived up to his expectations. Then, as he absentmindedly straightened some pencils on her desk, she saw that his hand was shaking and knew that he'd been as affected by what had occurred as she had. 'Fine,' she said lightly.

Jay gestured towards the clothes. 'Keep them here, you may need them again. I'll be back on Friday.' Then he was gone and Davina didn't understand why it was that she felt so let down.

'It isn't as though you were expecting him to leap on you,' she told herself crossly. 'A man like that isn't going to ask for sex as rent. He's playing with you, and you know it.' The trouble was, she was enjoying the game.

'Where are you off to?' Tanya asked Jay as she walked down the steps of the house. Her exotic beauty was set off to perfection by a simple flame-coloured linen shift, and her sunglasses were pushed up into her sleek black hair.

Not for the first time Jay felt slightly jealous of his boss. Tanya fascinated him and when they indulged in group sex he had some of his most intense orgasms with her. He still didn't believe that their marriage would last; Todd's record was hardly good in that respect, but for the moment he envied him his wife. 'I'm off to the village to get a few things, then I thought I'd have a pub lunch. Do you want to come too?'

She nodded. 'That sounds interesting. It will be my first English pub lunch.' They got into Jay's car.

'You gonna tell Todd?' queried Jay.

Tanya shook her head. 'I don't think he'll panic if I go missing for a couple of hours. You look very pleased with yourself,' she added, as the car pulled away from the house. 'What have you been up to?'

'What makes you think I've been up to anything? Maybe I'm simply feeling happy.'

'I didn't say you looked happy,' Tanya corrected him. 'I said you were looking pleased with yourself. There's a big difference. You may not be aware of it but you hardly ever look happy.'

'Is that a fact? I can assure you I often feel it.'

'Maybe, but not the kind of happy I'm thinking about.'

'I hope you're not going to try and sell me the advantages of wedded bliss,' teased Jay.

'Certainly not. I know very well what you think about marriage and I think everyone has to choose their own destiny.'

'But you think I'm missing out on something?'

'Yes,' she agreed. 'But I also think you're intelligent enough to realise it eventually.'

'How flattering.' Jay didn't feel flattered, in fact he was quite annoyed. Although there was only a year's difference between them, Tanya often succeeded in making Jay feel young. He found this difficult to handle because people normally thought he was older than his thirty years.

After he'd completed his shopping they adjourned to The Spreadeagle, a low-beamed pub full of polished brass ornaments, everything they had both expected from an English pub. Jay ordered steak and kidney pie but Tanya settled for a salad. 'So tell me,' she said quietly as she sipped her glass of wine. 'Why were you looking so pleased with yourself?'

'You don't give up, do you?' said Jay. 'It's no big deal. I went to the cottage to collect my rent that's all.'

He saw the expression in Tanya's eyes, and the strange yellow streaks that he sometimes detected at the height of sexual passion flickered there briefly for a moment. 'You mean you went to see Davina Fletcher?'

'She's the only tenant I've got.'

'I thought you said that she was paying her rent by acting as hostess for you.'

Jay nodded. 'True, but that only covered a few days. She was as surprised as you to realise that, but she understands the situation better now.'

Tanya frowned. 'I hope you're not being unkind to her, Jay.'

Jay sighed heavily. He always found it much easier talking to men than women because women got hooked on emotions, a trait he found irritating; he was happier with facts. 'What do you mean unkind?'

'Playing one of your games.'

'Well, yeah, I guess I am playing a game with her but she's enjoying it.'

'How do you know?'

'Believe me, I know. I remember my godfather telling me how worried he was when she first came to live in the cottage. He felt that she was shutting herself off from the world, that she wanted a permanent retreat, but that wasn't what he wanted for her. At first I couldn't imagine why he left me everything in the will, but I'm beginning to think he believed I could show Davina that there was more to life than estate agents and drawings.'

'How conceited!' exclaimed Tanya. 'Your godfather would probably have expected to live another twenty years. By then Davina would almost certainly have married her estate agent and you wouldn't have been in any position to make a difference to her life. Whatever it is that you're doing, don't try and justify it by saying it's what your godfather would have wanted.'

'Okay then, let's just say it's what I want. He left everything to me and his wording about the cottage rental was most specific.'

'He wasn't legally trained,' Tanya pointed out. 'He probably didn't expect you to take it quite so literally.'

Jay grinned. 'That's the beauty of it. To be truthful I didn't expect Davina to play along with me today. Since she did I'm assuming she's not averse to learning a bit more about herself.'

'Herself or her sexuality?' queried Tanya.

'Oh godammit!' said Jay. 'You and Todd spend most of your lives exploring your sexuality. Why is it that when I do it I get a lecture from you?'

'Sshh,' hissed Tanya. 'Everyone in the pub's looking at us.'

'I don't care. If they're rude enough to eavesdrop on a private conversation that's up to them.'

'You've got a very loud voice,' whispered Tanya. 'This isn't a courtroom and I'm not deaf. Neither, perhaps I should remind you, am I sitting in the dock.'

'You like me really though, don't you?' said Jay

quietly, putting his hand over hers. Her hand was very small and without thinking his fingers began to tighten around it. She responded by turning her palm uppermost and scratching lightly on the pads at the base of his fingers. The effect was electric. His blood raced and he felt himself stir. 'I take it that's a yes?'

'You know it's a yes,' she said with a smile. 'I just want you to realise that Davina isn't the only one who might be missing out on something. There is more to life than work and sex, Jay.'

'There is? Well, I sure as hell don't have time to fit it in.'

'You don't *want* to fit it in, that's the truth of it. Tell me about this morning then, what happened?'

Jay hesitated. It wasn't that Tanya would be shocked, in fact she'd probably find what had happened quite arousing, but all at once he didn't want her to know. He wanted it to remain a secret between himself and Davina, a secret that he knew would shame her, especially if she thought that there was any danger of him talking about it. 'I can't tell you,' he said slowly. 'If I did it would all be spoilt.'

Tanya pushed her plate away. 'That sounds interesting.'

'It is,' agreed Jay. 'Don't feel excluded, Tanya, I'm not going to tell Pattie either.'

Tanya gave him a very direct look. 'I imagine Pattie's the last person on earth you should tell.'

'Are you trying to make me feel guilty now?'

'Of course not, I don't believe in guilt. It's simply that Pattie might not appreciate you spending time alone with a young woman as attractive as Davina.'

'Pattie and I aren't engaged. I've never been faithful to her and I don't imagine she's faithful to me.'

'I think she is,' said Tanya.

Jay was astonished. The idea had never crossed his mind. 'You're joking?'

Tanya shook her head. 'She told me herself.'

'Why the hell's that?'

'Work it out for yourself, Jay.'

Jay groaned in mock despair. 'I can't possibly. I don't understand the way her mind works. I don't under-stand the way women's minds work, period.'

'I know you don't,' said Tanya. 'Mind you, you know more about a woman's body than any man I've met,' and she ran a foot up and down his trouser-leg beneath the table.

'More than Todd?'

Tanya nodded. 'Yes, more than Todd. Don't let that go to your head though, Jay. A woman sometimes wants more than a man who knows what buttons to push.'

'I'll remember that next time we're together,' said Jay teasingly.

Tanya looked fondly at him. 'When are we going to get together again, Jay?'

'All of us, you mean?' he asked. Tanya nodded. 'In about ten days. I hope you can wait that long.'

'Why the delay?' she asked curiously.

Jay stood up to go and pay the bill at the bar. 'Because there's some things I have to do before then, important things. I want it all to be right.'

'But it's always right,' said Tanya. 'I know Pattie's just as keen as Todd and me.'

'It's not Pattie I'm thinking about.' He was thinking about Davina.

The truth was, he was thinking about Davina far more than he wanted to and it was beginning to irritate him. It was fine when they were together, or when he was planning the next stage of the game, but throughout his lunch with Tanya her image kept appearing in his mind unbidden. This was something he wasn't used to.

He assumed it was because she was English, and intrinsically different to any other woman he'd known. Once the game was over and he'd actually possessed her he had no doubt that out of sight would be out of mind, just as it was with Pattie.

As he drove back home past the cottage, with Tanya sitting next to him, Jay gave two sharp blasts on the horn and saw Davina's face appear at the window for a fleeting second before she was lost to his. He smiled to himself. He would be there again on Friday.

When Davina heard a knock at her front door on the Friday morning her palms began to sweat. She knew without any doubt that it was Jay and her stomach seemed to shrink in on itself, the muscles clenching with a strange dark excitement. Opening the door she made certain that she stood in his way. This time if he wanted to come in he was going to have to ask.

Once again Jay had a cardboard box beneath his arm. 'May I come in?'

Davina felt as though she'd scored a point; at least she'd made him ask. 'Of course.' She stood to one side and his right arm brushed against her as he walked past. He was wearing a grey suit with a narrow stripe in it, a white shirt with a soft button-down collar and a dark red and green tie. He looked very formal, which somehow added to the excitement. It was such a contrast with what she knew was going to happen.

'I've come to watch you work again,' he said calmly. 'This is what I want you to wear today.'

Upstairs in her bedroom Davina drew out a black dress with narrow straps on the shoulders; it flared from just below the bust and ended a couple of inches above her knees. The underwear was also black, a half-cup strapless bra and a pair of lace panties cut high on the leg, far briefer than the cream ones she'd worn previously. This time the stockings were a golden shade of brown and had a soft sheen to them which caught the light. As she slipped her feet into the strappy leather sandals with the narrow high heels Davina could hardly breathe for excitement.

She hesitated at the entrance to her studio. 'Do you

want me just to draw again?' she asked at last when Jay stood watching her without uttering a word.

'Sure.'

'You bring me these clothes but you never say what you think of them,' Davina said suddenly, unable to stand his silence any longer.

'I like to keep my thoughts to myself. Just draw.'

She shivered. She'd never realised how erotic it was to be ordered around by a man, a man who she found incredibly attractive but who at the same time over-awed her. It was an amazingly arousing situation and her mouth felt dry. Sitting down on her stool she mois-tened her lips with the tip of her tongue and heard Jay draw in his breath sharply.

After she'd been drawing for about fifteen minutes he came and stood behind her and she felt his hands on the zip at the back of the dress. Automatically she stopped work and started to turn her head. 'Keep working,' he said sharply. 'I don't want you to do any-thing except draw.'

She could hardly grip the pencil her fingers felt so weak but obediently she remained with her head bowed over the board as Jay, agonisingly slowly, drew the zipper down. Then, just as she felt certain that he was going to touch her, he spoke. 'Slip the straps off.' His voice was thicker than usual but his tone was even. Uncertain as to exactly what he meant she looked questioningly at him as she slid the straps off her shoulders and down over her arms. As the dress fell forward into her lap, leaving her upper body clad only in the half-cup strapless bra, her breasts swelled and she felt the nipples thrusting against the material that was imprisoning them.

'Keep working,' he reminded her.

It was almost impossible. Davina felt like screaming at him, begging him to touch her, to do something to break the erotic tension that was building inside her, but he was in charge, he was the one who could choose what happened. All she could do was go along with his wishes. As she began to draw once more she felt tears prick her eyelids and bit hard on her lower lip. She was determined not to let him see how aroused and frustrated she was, even though she knew that he must guess. Suddenly she jumped as something cold touched her skin and she realised that he was fastening a pearl choker around her neck.

'Perfect,' he sighed, stepping away to study at her. 'Look at me, Davina.'

She raised her eyes from the drawing, and this time she didn't attempt to hide the hunger that she was feeling. 'Have you any idea how sexy you look?' he asked, but Davina knew that he didn't want an answer. He was really talking to himself.

Moving towards her he reached out and as she raised her head he drew the middle finger of his right hand in a line from the base of her throat, over her chest, finally coming to rest on the top of the bra. She was hardly breathing now, tense with expectation as his finger moved in two delicate arcs over the top half of each breast, tracing the outline of the bra. Her breasts were aching; she felt as though they were pulsating with her need.

'Stand up,' he ordered, removing his finger and stepping away from the desk.

Davina got to her feet and he signalled for her to walk around in front of him. Once more she obeyed and the silence in the room was electric. She could hear his breathing as well as her own. It was ragged, almost rasping, yet still he made no move towards her.

Davina wanted him. She'd never wanted anything so

much in her life before and it was shaming because she sensed that she was never going to have him. He was enjoying her need, taking pleasure from her frustration, and there was nothing she could do about it because it was impossible for her to hide her feelings.

'Does Phil have any idea how lucky he is?' he asked. She opened her mouth to reply but he crossed the room with two long strides and for one glorious moment his finger touched her lips. 'Don't bother to answer that. I know he doesn't. He isn't sophisticated enough to appreciate a woman like you.'

They were only two inches apart now and as he looked down at her, her lips parted involuntarily and she closed her eyes as his head moved a fraction as though he were about to kiss her. She was trembling with excitement, could already imagine how it would feel when his mouth closed over hers but then, to her shame, she felt him brush past her and heard the front door slam as he walked out.

She was left standing in her underwear, the black dress a crumpled heap by the stool where it had fallen to the floor when she'd stood up, and she was grateful that there'd been no one there to witness her humiliation as, with eyes closed, she'd craned forward for a kiss that Jay had never intended her to have.

Jay was just about to go into his study to work that afternoon when Pattie stopped him. 'Where were you this morning?' she asked.

'Examining my estate.'

Pattie didn't like the expression on her lover's face. 'What do you mean by that?'

'Precisely what I say. I always say what I mean, you should know that by now.'

'Which part of the estate?' she persisted, but then realised that she'd made a mistake as Jay frowned. 'Okay, if you don't want to tell me, don't. I can't imagine why it's such a big secret.'

'Anything else?' queried Jay.

Somehow Pattie managed to smile at him, when what she really felt like doing was screaming. 'No. Got a lot of work to do?'

'Afraid so. See you at dinner.'

Pattie turned and saw Tanya standing in the hallway. 'Why is he so secretive about everything?' she asked bitterly.

'Why do you want to know his every move?' asked Tanya gently.

'Because I want to be part of his life,' explained Pattie.

'Maybe that's not what he wants.'

'Maybe it's not, but it's what I intend to happen. I've just got to play my cards right that's all. I do love him you know.'

'I know you *think* you do,' agreed Tanya.

'I'm sure he was seeing Davina,' continued Pattie furiously. 'I can tell she fascinates him.'

'It's only because she's different and a challenge,' said Tanya soothingly. 'You're very tense, Pattie. Why don't I relax you a little?'

Pattie nodded. 'Sounds like a great idea. Let's use one of the guest rooms.'

In the small blue room, so called because of the varying shades of blue decoration, Pattie swiftly stripped off her tight white jeans and shocking pink top beneath which she wore nothing at all. Then she stretched herself out on the bed, her arms at her sides. 'Do anything you like,' she murmured. 'Whatever you do, it's always good.'

'I'll have to go and fetch a few things,' said Tanya, and for the few minutes that she was away Pattie couldn't help thinking about Davina and wondering what was going on in her lover's head.

However, all such thoughts were quickly wiped from her mind when Tanya delicately oiled Pattie's arms, shoulders and upper chest before starting to trail a vibrator over the flesh. She used the slow setting to lightly caress the delicate skin of the inside of Pattie's arms, moving around the crease of the armpit and up and down the arm. Then she applied it briefly to the tiny hollow at the base of Pattie's neck before repeating her movements on Pattie's other arm.

Pattie sighed. 'Such bliss,' she murmured. 'I wish Jay had the patience to do this sometimes.'

'Women understand women's bodies better,' said Tanya calmly. 'That doesn't mean it's better with women, just that it's different. Are you ready for a little more stimulation?' Pattie nodded, closed her eyes and parted her legs. She shivered as Tanya spread a little oil over the creases of her thighs and then, setting the vibrator to a faster speed, moved it swiftly across the skin before parting Pattie's sex lips and slowly easing it deep inside her until she was able to rotate it around the blonde girl's cervix. As usual this had a devastating effect on Pattie and with a scream of delight she climaxed, her whole body shuddering as wave after wave of contractions pulsed through her.

'God, that was good,' she groaned. 'Imagine how shocked Miss Prim at the cottage would be if she could see us now . . .'

'My turn,' said Tanya, handing the vibrator to Pattie.

'Wouldn't you just love to have her at our mercy for an hour or so?' asked Pattie, as she began to stimulate the Oriental girl.

'I'm not sure,' said Tanya slowly. 'Sometimes it's dangerous to introduce an outsider into a group when everything's going well. They can cause trouble.'

'Don't be silly,' said Pattie. 'Davina isn't the kind of girl to cause trouble.' But Tanya, already sighing with delight as the vibrator moved over her slender body, wasn't so sure.

Chapter Five

Phil arrived at the cottage early on the Saturday morning. 'Looks like I've brought the fine weather with me,' he said with a smile as Davina went out to greet him. 'They say today's going to be a real scorcher. It should be perfect for a dip in the lake.'

Davina frowned. 'I'm not sure if we can use the lake now.'

'Why not?'

'Because it belongs to Jay Prescott.'

'But we've always used the lake,' protested Phil.

'I've always used the lake,' Davina corrected him. 'You've been using it since we started going out together.'

'What's the difference? Have you asked Jay if you can have a swim?'

Davina remembered the way the American had studied her so intently as she'd sat, scantily clad, at her drawing board, her flesh trembling with desire. How could she possibly ask him for anything after that? 'I'd rather not.'

Phil groaned. 'You're pathetic. If you won't ask him I'll do it for you.'

'No!' Davina grabbed hold of Phil's arm. 'He might not want to let me use it, but he'll find it difficult to refuse me. If you ask he'll simply say no. He wouldn't feel that he owed it to Uncle David to let you swim in the lake.'

'Then ask him,' Phil urged her. 'I've been looking forward to a swim during the whole drive here. The traffic was appalling.'

'You didn't have to come.'

Phil looked sharply at her. 'Don't you want me here?'

'Yes, but not if the journey's such an ordeal for you. Besides, you never used to come every weekend.'

'It's different now,' he said truculently.

Davina was grateful that he didn't know exactly how

different it was. 'I'll go and ask him,' she said reluctantly. 'There's lemonade in the fridge when you've unpacked. Pour a glass for me will you, I won't be long.'

It was only as she walked up to the front door that she remembered that Jay had asked her to check with him before visiting the main house. Luckily it was Pattie who answered the door. 'Hi,' said the blonde girl, with a smile that didn't quite reach her eyes. 'What can I do for you?'

'Phil's here for the weekend,' explained Davina. 'When my uncle was alive we used to swim in the lake. I wondered if Jay would mind if we still did that?'

Pattie frowned. 'You swim in that horrible lake? The water's freezing!'

'We're not used to Californian sunshine, we're more willing to suffer for our pleasures, I suppose.'

'I don't know,' said Pattie hesitantly. 'Jay hasn't said anything about it and ...'

'What haven't I said anything about?' drawled Jay, looming up behind Pattie.

'Swimming in the lake.'

His eyes widened. 'Hell no, it's not something I've thought much about. I'm not into masochism.'

'Davina is,' said Pattie slyly, and Jay gave her an almost imperceptible shake of the head. Immediately she turned and walked away, leaving Davina wondering what the other girl had said wrong.

'You really want to swim in that thing, do you?' he queried.

She nodded. 'If you don't mind.'

'Why should I mind?'

'Because we'll be trespassing on your property.'

'We?'

'Phil's here for the weekend.'

He nodded. 'I see. I wondered what had given you the courage to make such a request. I got the feeling when I saw you last that you were a little on edge. When I heard your voice just now, I thought for one exciting moment that you'd come to invite me back to the cottage for another rent-paying session.'

Davina glanced at the ground. 'I'd rather not talk about that,' she muttered.

'I'm sure that's true,' he conceded. 'Don't worry, it's our little secret. As for the lake, feel free to take a dip whenever you like, providing you've no objection to me strolling over to take a look.'

'It's your lake,' said Davina.

Jay nodded. 'That's right, Davina. It's my lake, my house, and you're my tenant. I call the shots but as long as you ask nicely when you want something I think you might find that having me live here isn't too bad after all.'

'I must be getting back,' said Davina hastily, and for the first time that she could remember she heard Jay laugh softly as she turned her back on him and hurried back to the cottage.

'You took long enough,' said Phil. 'What did he say?'

'He doesn't mind at all. I don't think any of them will be using it. In America they like their water warmer.'

'You mean Pattie won't be swimming?' Phil sounded disappointed.

Davina laughed. 'From what she said I can't imagine anything less likely.'

'Have you seen much of her?' Phil tried to keep his voice casual but Davina sensed he was genuinely interested in the blonde girl. She remembered how the two of them had chatted together over dinner the previous weekend and wondered what they'd talked about.

'I haven't seen her at all. I've seen Jay once or twice but no one else.'

'Why have you seen Jay?'

Too late Davina realised that she should have kept quiet. 'He asked me to do a couple of bits of typing for him,' she lied.

'Oh, I see.' Phil promptly lost interest. 'What do you want to do after we've swum? Go into Oxford, take in a movie and then have a meal?'

'That sounds lovely. I'd like to get away from here for a bit.'

'It must be horrible for you,' said Phil sympathetically. 'If Jay was a different sort of person he'd be embarrassed at taking over the way he has, forcing you into the position of an outsider.'

'He didn't write the will, my uncle did,' said Davina quietly.

'I don't know why you stick up for him,' retorted Phil.

Davina didn't know either, but for some reason Jay always seemed much nicer when she was with Phil than when he was away. The contrast between them was so great that her tolerance of Phil plummeted to zero. 'Let's go and swim,' she said.

The lake was set at the far end of the grounds where the sloping lawn fell away and was surrounded by tall, thick bushes. These provided a good wind break and the whole area was quite a suntrap. Slipping off the skirt and blouse she'd put over her costume, Davina dived straight into the water then, as she surfaced, shrieked at the sudden coldness. 'It's freezing,' she shouted to Phil, who was still standing at the edge. He hesitated for a moment then dived in himself, but not as elegantly as Davina. It was more of a bellyflop than a dive and Davina, treading water nearby, saw that Pattie and Tanya, who were walking down the lawn, both started to laugh.

'We've got spectators,' she told Phil.

He looked over at the two women and waved cheerfully. 'Why don't you join us?' he shouted. As they reached the edge of the lake the two young women pretended to shiver and shook their heads. 'I can't swim,' explained Tanya, 'and Pattie likes her water warm.'

'Not like your men then,' shouted Phil.

Davina drew in her breath sharply. 'Be quiet,' she said in a low urgent voice. 'Jay might be around.'

'He isn't or we'd see him,' replied Phil. He swam

over to where Pattie was standing watching him, her large blue eyes alight with interest. 'Did you hear what I said?' he asked her.

Pattie nodded. 'I heard and you're right. I like my water warm and my men cold.'

'Doesn't sound very exciting.'

'They're not cold once I get them going. It's the cold exterior that fascinates me. I enjoy discovering the fires hidden beneath.'

'How deep do you have to go for that with your boyfriend?' asked Phil.

Davina couldn't believe what was going on. She felt horribly embarrassed. It was so rude, especially when Jay had allowed them to use the lake. 'Are you going to swim or not?' she asked Phil. 'I'll race you to the other side.' She turned her head to see if he'd taken up the challenge but he was still looking at Pattie.

'Perhaps I've got hidden fires,' she heard him murmur just before he started swimming.

When they got out of the water twenty minutes later the two girls had gone. 'How disappointing for you.' Davina's tone was acidic.

'What do you mean?'

'I heard what you were saying to her. Next time you and she want to flirt, perhaps you'd be polite enough to do it out of my sight.'

'It was only a bit of fun.'

'Is that what you call it? Seemed like more than that to me.'

As she talked Davina was pulling crossly at her swimsuit, peeling it off her damp skin and wondering why it was that swimsuits were so difficult to remove. As she stepped out of it and reached down for the towel she realised, too late, that Jay was standing on the top of the slope looking down at them and holding a pair of binoculars to his eyes. Terrified that Phil would notice she rubbed briskly at herself with the towel, then dressed so quickly that for the first time in living memory she was ready before Phil.

'What's got into you?' he asked in astonishment. Then he smiled. 'I know what it is, you're feeling sexy, aren't you? You want to go back to the cottage.'

Davina nodded. She certainly did want to go back to the cottage. She also wanted Jay to go back to the house, now, before Phil saw him. 'That's right,' she said weakly.

'Suits me,' agreed Phil. 'You know, lately our sex life's gone off a bit but I've got a feeling things are going to perk up again.'

'Uncle David's death did affect me,' Davina pointed out.

'I know, I know and I didn't make enough allowances but this weekend we'll make up for it.'

The adrenaline rush caused by swimming in the cool lake, coupled with the knowledge that Jay had seen her totally naked and unknowingly exposed to him, had combined to make Davina feel extremely sexy. She ran up the stairs of the cottage laughing as Phil pursued her, and once in the bedroom turned the chair in front of her dressing table so that it was facing towards the bed. She then started to undress, letting her clothes fall in a heap at her feet.

'What do you want me to do?' asked Phil.

Davina wished that he hadn't asked, wished that he'd simply taken command in the way that Jay took command whenever he was watching her draw. Then she banished the treacherous thought from her mind, reasoning that comparisons were unfair. Jay was playing games with her but Phil loved her, or at least was fond of her. They had a proper relationship and it wasn't his fault that she found the enigmatic American more fascinating. 'Sit naked on the chair and I'll sit on top of you,' she explained.

'You're different you know,' said Phil, as she planted her feet firmly on the floor before lowering herself gradually onto his erection, her hands gripping the sides of his neck while his arms went around her waist. 'You'd never have wanted to do this a few months ago.'

'We all change,' she whispered, slowly moving herself up and down on him. 'Use your mouth on me,' she added.

Phil drew back and stared at her. 'I'm not sure I like it when you give orders.'

'I'm not giving orders, I'm just saying what I'd like you to do. Surely you want to give me pleasure?'

'I always give you pleasure, don't I?'

She didn't answer but simply lifted her breasts so that Phil had little choice but to bend his head and fasten his lips around the tender flesh while Davina, her chin resting on the top of his head, stared at herself in the dressing table mirror.

She couldn't remember ever feeling so excited. As

her body moved up and down and the delicious tightness began deep inside her, she watched herself,
watched her cheeks suffuse with colour and her eyes
start to glow. She wished that Phil would do more, use
his hands to help lift her body up and down, or draw
one of her nipples fully into his mouth rather than licking lightly around them but she didn't dare say
anything. Instead, to her shame, she started to imagine
that it was Jay seated on the chair, Jay she was seduc-
ing, bringing to a climax as she rhythmically
contracted her internal muscles and felt the delicious
fullness inside her.

'If you keep doing that I shall come too soon,' muttered Phil. Davina knew that she was working her
muscles too hard, but she didn't want to stop because
every time she contracted them tiny pinpricks of pleasure shot through her pubic mound and into her lower
belly, increasing the sexual tension as her orgasm drew
ever nearer. Realising that Phil wasn't going to last
much longer she allowed herself to fantasise even more
about Jay, while at the same time speeding up her body
movements until suddenly it was happening.

She felt the pressure increase, felt her belly swell and

her muscles tighten in anticipation. 'Yes! Yes!' she whispered, but her words, spoken without thought, proved fatal because it was Phil who came, groaning despairingly as his fingers dug into the flesh each side of her spine, and shaking spasmodically beneath her.

Davina was stranded, perched on the very edge of her orgasm, desperate for relief. She couldn't believe that this was happening to her, not when it had all been going so well and she lifted herself up so that Phil could slide out of her before pushing one of his hands down between her thighs. 'Use your fingers on me,' she implored him.

'Haven't you come?' He sounded quite aggrieved.

Davina couldn't believe that he didn't know. 'Not yet, please, hurry up.'

With obvious reluctance Phil's fingers parted her sex lips and moved indolently up and down the frantic inner channel, finally brushing against the side of her swollen clitoris. At last, almost despite her lover, she came and the delicious pleasure swamped her.

'My thighs are aching,' complained Phil. 'If you've finished you'd better get off me. I still think we'd have been more comfortable on the bed.'

'But it made such a nice change,' said Davina.

'It was obvious you felt more in command.'

'I'm sorry, I didn't realise you wouldn't like it. I thought it would be exciting for both of us.'

'It was all right,' he conceded.

Later, when they drove into town, there was an awkwardness between them that even Davina's best attempts at conversation couldn't quite disguise. When they returned at eight o'clock that evening she was so worn out with the strain of trying to pretend that everything was all right that she was almost relieved when Phil said someone should walk the dog.

'I'm too tired,' she murmured.

'It's all right, I don't mind going alone,' he assured her.

Davina smiled at him. 'Thanks, that's really helpful.'

'I'm glad I'm good for something.'

Davina sighed. Phil was right, she was changing and it was Jay who was changing her, but she was sure that a lot of men would have thought she was changing for the better. She wondered why Phil didn't appreciate it.

Sitting in the swing seat at the rear of the house, enjoying the evening sunshine, Pattie sighed.

'Something wrong?' queried Jay, who was sitting next to her with a pile of legal papers on his knees.

'I'm bored.'

'Then find something to do. I've got a lot to read before I go to London next week.'

'How long will you be away?'

'I'm not sure.'

'What am I going to do?' She tried not to sound aggrieved but knew that she'd failed when Jay shot her an irritated glance.

'I'm sure you, Todd and Tanya can provide your own entertainment. I thought you wanted to learn how to run an English country house while we were here?'

'Clive won't let me,' Pattie complained.

'He's an employee,' Jay pointed out. 'He can't stop you doing anything.'

Pattie didn't contradict Jay, but he was wrong. Clive was clever enough not to show his contempt for Pattie in front of his new employer, but when they were alone together he'd discovered many ways of making it plain to Pattie. The problem was, he was never rude, never said anything that she could take exception to, but his contempt for her was there just the same, concealed beneath the polite veneer of an English manservant.

She knew that Todd and Tanya were watching a sex movie but she didn't want to join them, not without Jay. The three of them would have enough time together next week. 'Couldn't we have some fun?' she suggested, running a hand up the side of Jay's thigh.

He moved slightly, making his displeasure clear. 'I'm not going to tell you again, I'm busy.'

'Well, I'm going for a walk!' she exclaimed.

'Fine.'

She walked away from him as provocatively as she could, knowing that her tight skirt would emphasise the sway of her buttocks as she placed one high-heeled shoe in front of the other. It would turn Jay on, and serve him right, she thought to herself. He'd positively neglected her recently and she suspected she knew the reason why. The last time he'd been to the cottage to 'collect his rent', as he put it, she'd suggested that she went with him, but he'd refused and her suspicions had turned to certainty. He was intrigued by Davina, and although Pattie thought that the English girl was too boring to hold his attention for long she was still watchful. With a country estate in England to go with his position in Boston society Jay was now an even better catch than before, and she didn't intend to lose him. On the other hand, she wasn't going to let him take her for granted.

She kept walking until she reached the summerhouse and there, coming from the opposite direction, she saw Davina's boyfriend Phil, a black Labrador dog racing around in circles near him.

'If that dog messes on the lawn Jay'll have him shot,' she called.

Phil drew level with her. 'That would suit me.'

She was surprised but also intrigued. 'I thought the English were passionate about their dogs?'

'This isn't my dog, it was Davina's uncle's.'

'Right. You're not a dog man I take it?'

'No, I prefer blonde Californian girls.'

'To lead around on a leash?' she asked mischievously.

For a moment he looked startled and she realised that things she now took for granted because of Jay would be totally alien to this stolid estate agent. She studied him carefully. He was not quite as tall as Jay, probably a fraction under six foot, and was sturdily built with fair wavy hair. His blue eyes lacked the penetration of Jay's gaze but there was a remoteness about them that intrigued her. Suddenly she thought of a way to relieve her boredom.

'Get rid of the dog,' she murmured huskily, moving closer to Phil.

'How?'

'Tell it to go home or something.'

'I don't know if that'll work,' he muttered, turning towards the barking dog. 'Home boy,' he said firmly, and to Pattie's relief the dog immediately started running towards the cottage.

'There, problem solved,' she said brightly, and holding out her hand she drew Phil towards the steps that led up to the summerhouse. She could tell that he was both excited and nervous, which only increased her own desire. Within seconds she'd stripped and promptly started to unfasten Phil's jeans. For a moment he put his hand on hers as though he was going to push her away, but then with a groan of desire he allowed her to ease his zip down and within seconds was tearing at his own shirt as her urgency communicated itself to him.

The evening sun was shining down on them and

Pattie's flesh revelled in the warmth. She lay on her back on the steps, her right leg bent at the knee, her left extended straight in front of her. When Phil hesitated she reached up and pulled him down over her so that his hands were resting on the top step above her head, his right knee was next to her face, his left leg placed between her thighs.

Now Pattie was able to take him into her mouth, to draw in the long lean length of him while at the same time she used her hands to stimulate the root of his erection. She heard him give a sigh of pleasure and pressed her right thigh against his left leg, reminding him that she too needed stimulation.

Phil moved his leg between her thighs, pushing hard against her pubic mound while she wriggled her hips as the first exciting tremors began to shake her body. She felt wonderful. She could tell from the smothered gasps that were coming from Phil that he was unbearably excited and she deliberately stopped sucking on his glans, deciding instead to use her tongue lightly and teasingly around the soft ridge, occasionally flicking it into the slit at the top without ever quite allowing him to come.

Half mad with excitement and need, Phil pressed his leg even harder against Pattie's sex and she felt her clitoris being stimulated as the outer sex lips pressed down on it. She whimpered with pleasure and while continuing to massage Phil's erection with her left hand used her right to caress her own breasts. She pinched the nipples and surrounding areolae so that streaks of pleasure shot through her, down between her ribs and into her belly. She knew that they were both rapidly approaching their climax and now, because her own orgasm was imminent, she started to suck slowly and steadily on Phil's erection again.

'God, that feels good,' he moaned.

Pattie felt a surge of power. When she was with Jay he was always the one in control, calling the shots, and normally she liked that but this was deliciously different. Slowly the wonderful sensations drew together, pulling her muscles tightly in on themselves, then she felt her body explode in an ecstasy of sexual release and writhed helplessly as the waves of pleasure swamped her.

Just as her orgasm was finishing Phil's began. Suddenly he started thrusting himself deep inside her mouth, and she felt the delicious hot fluid pumping out of him.

'Enjoying yourselves?' asked an all-too-familiar voice.

Pattie hastily swallowed the last drops that had spilt from Phil and then sat up, her face flushed, her body still shaking with the aftermath of pleasure. Although shocked, she was glad that Jay had seen them because now he must surely realise that he couldn't simply ignore her or treat her casually. He'd understand that other men found her attractive too, and she waited for his anger to explode.

'I said, are you enjoying yourselves?'

Pattie saw that Phil had hurried into the summer-house, slamming the door behind him, unable to face the American while nude and vulnerable. 'Yes thank you,' she said pertly.

Jay nodded. 'I thought you were.'

'It just happened,' she explained.

'You don't have to apologise. You're a free agent.'

'But ...'

'You'd better put your clothes on now though,' continued Jay smoothly. 'The sun's going down and you don't want to catch a cold.' With that he walked calmly away as though nothing unusual had happened, leaving Pattie stunned by his indifference.

'Has he gone?' hissed Phil, sticking his head round the summerhouse door.

'Yes.'

'Did he see it was me?'

'I don't suppose he thought it was Father Christmas.'

'Oh God, what am I going to do?' exclaimed Phil. 'He might throw Davina out and she'll never forgive me.'

'For what, having her thrown out of the cottage or for having sex with me?'

'Both.'

'I don't think you need worry,' said Pattie shortly. 'Jay wasn't bothered.'

'What do you mean?' Phil looked astonished.

'Just what I said, he wasn't bothered.'

Phil frowned. Clearly the situation was beyond him. 'I must get back,' he muttered. 'Davina will be wondering where I am.'

'Did you enjoy it?' asked Pattie, stretching sensuously, and watching Phil's eyes flicker towards her perfect breasts.

'Of course I did. It was the most fantastic sex I've ever had.'

Pattie felt a glow of satisfaction. Even if Jay's reaction had been disappointing, Phil's wasn't. He looked like an adolescent who'd just discovered the joys of sex and that made her feel extra good. 'Then we must do it again,' she said, getting to her feet and slowly dressing herself, making sure that Phil saw every inch of her in the process.

'That would be fantastic! The only problem is Davina. I wouldn't want to hurt her.'

'Don't worry, I won't tell if you don't,' Pattie assured him.

'Of course I won't.' He went to kiss her but Pattie turned her head away.

'Time to go back to the girlfriend,' she reminded him with a laugh, and set off for the main house leaving him staring besottedly after her.

Todd, Tanya and Jay were all waiting for her in the drawing room when she got back. 'I have to say I had no idea you were that bored,' remarked Jay. 'I suppose I should be grateful you didn't ask Clive to accompany you to the summerhouse.'

'It wasn't an assignation,' said Pattie. 'We just happened to meet. You know how these things happen.'

Jay nodded. 'I certainly do. Not very chivalrous is he, your Englishman? He shot off into the summerhouse like a startled rabbit.'

'He was afraid you were going to hit him, or even worse turn Davina out of her cottage.'

Jay frowned. 'Why should I turn Davina out of her cottage because her boyfriend's having sex with you?'

'Because you were annoyed and jealous, I suppose.'

'Jealous?' He looked genuinely astounded. 'Why the hell should I be jealous?'

'Most men would be.'

'I'm not most men. Anyway, I assume you both had a good time and since the pair of you are over the age of consent it really doesn't concern anyone else, does it?'

Pattie looked at Tanya. 'Can you believe this guy? He finds me making passionate love to someone else and isn't even bothered.'

'You make love to Todd in front of him and that doesn't bother him. He was hardly likely to be shocked,' said Tanya gently.

'That's different,' said Pattie, her voice rising. 'We all share each other. Phil's an outsider.'

'You sound as though you only did it to make me jealous,' remarked Jay.

'Don't be ridiculous. I did it because I wanted to.'

'Good, because I never play the jealousy game.'

'Talking of playing games,' Todd interrupted, 'when are we all gonna play?'

'Good question,' murmured Jay. 'As you know I've got to go to London on Monday afternoon. A friend of my father's has managed to get me into the Old Bailey for the week so that I can see the way the British judicial system works at the very highest level. I won't be back until Friday night but I thought we'd have one of our games on Sunday.'

Tanya smiled. 'How lovely. It's been ages since we all got together like that. Have we got a theme?'

'I thought voyeurism,' said Jay.

'Voyeurism?' queried Pattie. 'I'm not going to simply watch everyone. I like taking part.'

'Hell, we all like taking part,' said Todd. 'Which one of us do you think is going to be willing to sit it out, Jay?'

'None of us,' said Jay slowly.

'Then how can it be the theme?' asked Tanya.

'I'm going to get Davina to watch.'

There was a sudden silence in the room and Pattie glanced over at Tanya, opened her mouth to protest but then closed it again as Tanya shook her head in a silent warning. Pattie wanted to shout at Jay, to tell him that this wasn't right, that Davina didn't belong in their games, but she couldn't because she was only one of the players. It was Jay who made up the rules.

'Is that wise?' asked Todd.

'You don't think I'm old enough to know what I'm doing?' queried Jay, an edge to his voice.

'Sure, you always know what you're doing,' Todd said amiably. 'I'm just not certain Davina will enjoy it.'

'Don't worry, I'm not going to lock her up and keep her prisoner. She'll be free to leave if she wants to, but my guess is she'll stay.'

'What are you going to do, send her an invitation?' asked Pattie sarcastically.

'Don't concern yourself about it,' said Jay. 'You weren't worried about Davina when you were sucking her boyfriend off, so why the concern now? I shall set it all up in my own way but I don't expect any of you to give away any secrets. It's to come as a surprise to her. I want to see her reaction when she realises the kind of things we do.'

'Could be interesting,' agreed Todd.

Pattie was livid. This was what she'd dreaded, the gradual encroachment of Davina into their lives, but now, after being caught in the grounds with Phil, she was in no position to argue. All she could do was wait and hope; wait to see how Jay lured Davina into the house, and hope that once she saw what was going on, she left.

'I still don't understand how you lost Major,' persisted Davina as she and Phil got into bed that night.

'I told you, he ran off after a rabbit or something and I thought he'd doubled back towards the lake. It never occurred to me that he might have come back to the cottage. After all, he hasn't lived here long. It seemed more likely to me that he'd have tried to go into the main house.'

'Did you go there and ask if they'd seen him?' asked Davina.

Phil shook his head. 'No.'

Davina was baffled. She'd been surprised when Major had arrived home off the lead and without any sign of Phil, but her surprise had turned to anxiety when an hour passed and Phil still hadn't returned.

Then, when he finally did, he'd seemed strange and acted as though he had some kind of guilty secret. She couldn't believe that he'd tried to lose the dog. Even though he wasn't particularly fond of it, he wouldn't have done something like that, so she couldn't make out what he was hiding.

'You haven't had a row with Jay, have you?' she asked suddenly.

Phil flushed. 'About what?'

'I don't know, anything. You're always saying how you dislike him. Please, tell me that you didn't row with him. I'd never forgive you if I lost this cottage because of you.'

She was certain that she again saw guilt in Phil's eyes for a moment but then he turned his back on her and settled down to sleep. 'Don't be ridiculous. Of course I didn't have a row with Jay. I'd never do anything to jeopardise you keeping this cottage, surely you know me better than that.'

'But you're hiding something from me,' persisted Davina. 'You're a hopeless liar, Phil, you always have been. Come on, tell me what it is.'

'If you must know I was watching those two women. They were both sitting on the summerhouse steps with next-to-nothing on and I watched them from the copse opposite. Pathetic, isn't it? I wasn't going to tell you because I was thoroughly ashamed of myself, but since you've kept on and on about it you might as well know the truth.'

Davina felt nothing but relief. 'Is that all? I wish you'd told me earlier.'

'I thought you'd go mad.'

Davina nearly laughed. Compared with what Jay made her do, Phil watching Pattie and Tanya was nothing but she couldn't tell him that. 'I know you like Pattie,' she murmured, as she too settled down to sleep. 'I don't blame you, she's a very pretty girl.'

'What do you mean, like her?' demanded Phil, propping himself up on one elbow. 'I hope you're not suggesting that I fancy her.'

Davina was surprised at his reaction. 'Yes, I think you do fancy her a little, but it doesn't bother me.

Hardly likely to come to anything, is it? I don't blame you for looking, most men would.'

'Why do you say it won't come to anything?'

'What are you on about?' asked Davina in surprise. 'I assume it won't come to anything because you're with me. I mean, you are faithful to me, aren't you? Or isn't Pattie the first blonde girl who's caught your eye since we've been together?'

'Of course I'm faithful to you,' said Phil, putting his head back on the pillow. 'I thought you were trying to say that a girl like that wouldn't be interested in me.'

'No that wasn't what I meant,' said Davina sleepily. 'Mind you, I don't imagine that she would be.'

Within a few minutes she could hear Phil snoring slightly and knew that he was asleep. Unfortunately sleep didn't come so easily to her. She realised that she was already anticipating Monday morning, when Jay would call to collect his rent. She wondered what would happen this time, how far he would go. Would he allow her frantic body any kind of satisfaction, or did he intend to keep her in a state of sexual frustration and desire? In the end she supposed it didn't really matter, the only thing that mattered was that he came.

Chapter Six

On the Monday morning Davina waited excitedly for Jay. She was certain that this time he *would* touch her because it seemed a natural progression. She sensed that for him part of the pleasure of the game was the slow pace at which he was taking his strange seduction, but when he finally arrived her spirits sank. It was clear from his dark formal suit and the fact that his car was parked in the drive that he wasn't intending to stay.

'Did you want to come in?' she asked.

'Your eagerness is flattering. Unfortunately I gotta go to London for the week.'

Davina felt very angry, both with herself and with

him. 'I wasn't being eager, I was being polite,' she said icily.

'I will come in for a few minutes, there's something I need to talk to you about.'

Thoroughly annoyed, Davina decided that he could sit in the kitchen. Unfortunately it didn't seem to faze him at all and he sat without hesitation on one of the small wooden chairs, despite the fact that he was really too large for it. 'I'll be at the Old Bailey all this week,' he began.

'They've found you out, have they?'

He gave a thin smile. 'I'm going to be studying your judicial system. It should be interesting. I can always discuss it with your boyfriend the next time we meet.'

'What did you need to talk to me about?' asked Davina, determined not to be side-tracked by his small-talk.

'When I come back I wanna hold a dinner party for four at the main house. Sunday night would be best.'

'That's for you, Pattie, Todd and Tanya, is it?' enquired Davina.

'Did I say that?'

'No, but I assumed ...'

'Never assume anything. I want you to choose all your favourite dishes for the menu. I guess Phil will be here that weekend?'

Davina nodded. She wondered what an evening spent in the company of Jay, Pattie and Phil would be like. Exhilarating probably, and far more intimate than when the other two Americans had been present. All at once her excitement, previously subdued when she learnt he was going away, began to rise again. 'It'll be a pleasure.'

Jay nodded. 'I thought it would. We'll dine at eight-thirty. I'm sure you and the cook can get everything organised before I get back Friday night.'

'I'll leave a copy of the menu at the main house for you,' said Davina.

'Great! See you next weekend then.'

'I hope you manage to learn something while you're away,' said Davina, walking to the front door with him.

'I make a point of learning something every day.'

'How noble,' remarked Davina. 'That sounds like something you'd find in a fortune cookie.'

'I did see it in a fortune cookie.' He laughed, and with that he was gone.

The week flew by. She was coming to the end of the sci-fi drawings and knew that soon she'd have to send them off to the publisher. As the deadline drew nearer so the pressure on her increased. At the same time she worked hard to make sure that the Sunday dinner party was perfect down to the last detail, even arranging the decor for the table settings.

Clive was clearly delighted to be working alongside her again and they talked fondly of Uncle David. Clive surprised her with tales of the dead man's travels. 'He was very popular with the ladies, you know,' he said at one point and Davina was surprised because she'd always considered Uncle David a dry old bachelor. Perhaps that was why he felt she was missing out on life, she thought, but it was different for men.

Occasionally when she was at the main house she bumped into Todd or Tanya, but she never saw Pattie. Todd was very friendly and Davina liked him, particularly his enthusiasm; he was so different from Jay, completely open and up-front. It was easy to forget that he was Jay's boss because his whole approach to life was far more laid back and less intense.

Finally it was Saturday. Davina sent the art work

recorded delivery from the local post office, and got back to the cottage just as Phil arrived. 'We've been invited to dinner at the main house tomorrow night,' she told him after they'd kissed. She fully expected him to complain but he looked pleased.

'Good. Will it be the six of us, or are other people coming?'

'It's only four of us.'

'Which four?'

'Jay and Pattie, you and me.'

Phil frowned. 'Why not Todd and Tanya?'

'I've no idea,' confessed Davina. 'Anyway, he told me to pick all my favourite dishes and I made sure that they were things that you like too.'

'In other words the food will be good even if the company's crap.'

'The company won't be crap,' said Davina. 'I thought you liked Pattie.'

'She's okay,' murmured Phil. 'Did you get your work off?' he continued. It was so unusual for him to take any interest in her work that Davina didn't ask any more questions about Pattie but instead started discussing the drawings.

Early that evening as she and Phil were kissing on the couch, and just as Phil's hands had started to move up beneath her T-shirt, the phone went. 'Blast,' he muttered. 'Let it ring.'

'I can't,' said Davina. 'I won't be able to concentrate.' She heard Phil sigh as she went into the kitchen and picked up the phone. 'Hello?'

'Hi, I'm back,' said Jay's familiar voice.

'How nice.'

'Don't sound too enthusiastic, will you. I'd like you to come across, we need to discuss tomorrow.'

'Now?'

'Yeah, now. Pattie and I always have a lie-in on Sunday mornings, if you get my drift.'

'I get your drift,' she said hurriedly. 'I'll be right over.'

'Where the hell are you going?' demanded Phil as she picked up a sweater.

Davina sighed. 'Over to the main house. Jay's back and wants to discuss tomorrow's meal.'

'Can't he wait?'

'It seems not. Even the slow progress of the English law courts hasn't taught him patience.'

'Well, don't be long.'

'I won't,' promised Davina.

'Nice to see you don't feel you have to dress up for me,' remarked Jay, opening the front door of the house.

'You wanted me to come over at once and this is what I was wearing when you rang,' retorted Davina.

'Sure, like I said, I'm glad you feel relaxed enough to let it all, what's the expression, hang out?'

At that moment Pattie drifted by wearing a long tight-fitting dress, her blonde hair piled high on her head and the fragrance of an expensive perfume all around her. She made Davina feel like a grubby child.

'Why ask me over now if you're about to go out?' she asked.

'We're not going out, we like to dress up from time to time. Most women enjoy that, I believe.'

'I didn't organise a special dinner for tonight,' Davina said awkwardly.

'We're not eating, we're playing cards.'

She couldn't help but look surprised. 'Cards?'

'Sure, we all get dressed up and then play strip poker.'

She didn't know whether he was joking or not, but she saw Pattie give her lover a seductive smile as she walked towards the billiard room and at that moment Davina decided that Jay was telling the truth. She wondered what it must be like to share your life with a man like him. It would frighten her, but at the same time she couldn't help being turned on by the idea.

'Did you hear what I said?' demanded Jay.

Davina jumped. 'Sorry! I was miles away.'

'So I saw. I can't find the menu for tomorrow night. You had said you were going to leave me a copy.'

'It's in the kitchen, stuck to the pantry door.'

'Are you sure?'

'Positive.'

'Show me,' said Jay, and he stepped back so that Davina could lead the way. She could feel him right behind her; it was as though they were back at the cottage and he was watching her, despite the fact that this time she was fully clothed.

'There you are,' she said, pointing at the list.

'Now how the hell did I miss that?' he asked casually.

'I've no idea.' Davina's voice was stiff with annoyance. Clearly he had seen it, he'd simply called her over there for his own amusement, probably so that she could see Pattie and learn what was going on in the main house that evening.

'It looks great,' said Jay, running his eyes over the page. 'I'm sure Tanya will love the lime dessert.'

'Tanya?' asked Davina in surprise.

'You have a problem with that?'

'No, but I didn't think Tanya and Todd were going to be at the dinner.'

'And who did you think the meal was for?'

Davina felt incredibly uncomfortable. 'It doesn't matter,' she murmured.

'Hey, tell me. You must have had someone in mind.'

'I thought ... That is, because you asked me to choose my favourite foods and ... '

'And?'

'And you implied that Todd and Tanya weren't going to be the guests, I'd assumed that Phil and I were joining you and Pattie.'

Jay's face was expressionless. 'You really thought I'd want to spend the evening in the company of your boyfriend without another man there. What kind of conversation was that going to provide?'

'I'm sorry, it was a misunderstanding.'

'It sure as hell was. I hope you haven't mentioned it to Phil.'

'Oh God!' Davina's hand flew to her mouth.

'I take it that means you have. Well, not only are you gonna have to tell him that he ain't invited, you're also gonna have to tell him you'll be over here serving us because it's Jenny's night off.'

Davina's cheeks were scarlet, and she felt as though her skin was burning. She was absolutely mortified. 'You want me to wait at table?'

'That's right.'

'I'm not a servant.'

'Careful, Davina,' he said quietly. 'If you remember I wasn't able to collect my rent on Monday because I had to go to London. I'm collecting it tomorrow night instead.'

'You needn't think I'm serving you wearing just underwear,' she said angrily, certain that this must be his intention and knowing that if it was she had to refuse, even if it meant losing the cottage.

He looked surprised. 'What do you think I am, some kinda weirdo? A dark skirt and white blouse

will be fine. I trust that won't make you feel too sub-
servient?'

'I think I can cope with that,' she mumbled.

'Excuse me?'

Davina raised her voice. 'I said, I think I can cope
with that.'

'Good. We'll need you over here about seven-thirty.
You can help in the kitchen first and generally assist in
getting it all together. Any questions?'

Davina shook her head. She knew that he'd planned
this deliberately. He'd known perfectly well that he was
misleading her, that she was bound to assume she and
Phil were to be the guests. Now he was taking a per-
verse pleasure in her embarrassment and confusion. She
was furious, and she knew that Phil would be furious
too but she had no choice. She wanted to remain in the
cottage and Jay knew that only too well.

'What do you mean I'm not invited?' Phil shouted
incredulously. 'I thought you said we were the only
guests?'

'I was confused,' said Davina. 'I misunderstood what
Jay said.'

'You mean you're invited and I'm not?'

'No, it's not like that at all. I'm only going there to serve at table. It's Jenny's night off.'

'You're not a servant.'

'I don't have any choice,' said Davina quietly. 'I'm sure you haven't forgotten the wording of the will. Jay wants me to help out so that's what I've got to do.'

'And what am I supposed to do?'

'I won't be gone long. Dinner's at eight-thirty so it should all be over by say half-ten, eleven.'

'I'm not sitting here on my own for the evening waiting until you've washed the last of the dishes. You're a talented artist, Davina. Don't you think perhaps you ought to consider leaving here?'

Davina couldn't believe her ears. 'Leave here? I couldn't possibly.'

'Why not?'

'Because it's my home.'

'It isn't,' said Phil irritably. 'You're renting the cottage from a man you hardly know and he can throw you out at any moment simply by making some ridiculous request of you. It's hardly a safe existence, Davina, and I know how much importance you place on safety.'

'I'm not leaving because Uncle David never intended me to leave. If you don't like what's happening then don't bother to come and see me any more.'

'Are you saying you've had enough of me?'

'Of course not, although sometimes I don't think that you feel the same about me now you know I'm not the heiress to a vast estate.'

Phil had the grace to look slightly abashed. 'I mind for you, Davina, not for myself.'

'So what are you going to do on Sunday?'

'Drive back to London. I'd thought of going back late Sunday night in any case. This has decided me.'

'I'm sorry,' said Davina softly. 'I really did think that Jay intended us to be his guests.'

Phil laughed. 'I'm not surprised you got confused. Americans don't speak English properly. Let's go up, Davina. We might not have tomorrow evening, but we've still got tonight.'

'I'm not certain this is a great idea,' said Todd Lattimer to Tanya as the pair of them dressed for dinner the following evening. 'What's to stop Davina leaving as soon as she realises what's happening?'

'Jay seems certain she'll stay,' murmured Tanya, clipping the two ends of a gold chain onto each of her nipples before slipping on her satin blouse. 'I assume he knows what he's talking about.'

'His judgement's usually pretty sound,' agreed Todd. 'What do you think of Davina?'

'I hardly know her,' said Tanya, wrapping the sarong style black ankle-length skirt around her waist. 'She seems nice. She's classy, and intelligent too. If she was American I'd say she was the ideal partner for Jay.'

'Yeah, but she's a Brit, and in any case he isn't looking for an ideal partner. He's looking for an exciting sexual adventure.'

'She doesn't look like an exciting sexual adventure to me,' confessed Tanya. 'But we'll have to wait and see.'

'How does Pattie feel about all this?'

Tanya pulled a face. 'She's pretty fed up. She told me that when Jay caught her and that fair-haired boyfriend of Davina's screwing on the steps of the summerhouse, he didn't react at all. She's certain that's because he's got designs on Davina. I think she planned it to make him jealous, but now she feels she's given him carte blanche to do as he likes with Davina.'

'You'd think Pattie would know it's a waste of energy trying to make Jay jealous,' said Todd. 'It's like in court when people try to get him to lose his temper. It's impossible. That guy's more in control of himself than anyone I've ever met. The problem is, he likes to control everyone else as well.'

'That can be exciting,' murmured Tanya.

'Sure, and I know how much you enjoy these evenings of ours, but he's a bit cold for a proper relationship, wouldn't you say?'

'He seems cold,' said Tanya thoughtfully. 'I wonder, if tonight goes the way Jay wants, whether you and I could give Davina a helping hand.'

'In what way?'

'You know, give her hints on the way to his heart.'

'Has he got one?'

'Of course he has, it's just that no one's found it yet. Maybe Davina's the one to do that.'

'Yeah, and maybe she's not. Come on, time for us to go down. Next thing you know Jay will be ticking us off for being late for pre-dinner drinks.' They both laughed and made their way to the study where Clive was standing behind the small bar that Jay had had built. Pattie, wearing an ice-blue silk dress that left one shoulder bare, shimmied over to greet them.

'Have you heard, Davina's going to be waiting on us?'

'We'd heard,' said Todd. 'How do you feel about that?'

Pattie shrugged. 'I don't see the point, but Jay's excited about it.'

'Is he getting her to dress up in a maid's uniform?' asked Todd eagerly.

Pattie shook her head. 'No, nothing like that. It must be part of his plan to involve her. You know Jay, once he gets an idea in his head that's it.'

For a while the two young women talked together while Todd and Jay discussed Jay's week in London. The sound of a gong being struck finally interrupted their conversations and the four of them went through to the dining room.

The moment they'd sat down Davina walked into the room carrying four bone china bowls of consommé which she placed in front of each of them. She then went to leave the room but Jay held up a hand.

'Don't leave, wait there behind Todd. That way you can clear the plates as soon as we've finished.' Davina obediently stood by the wall, only moving when the bowls were empty.

With the main course of pork cooked with English vegetables and mixed herbs in front of them, the four Americans, relaxed by the excellent wine Jay had provided, began to discuss American politics. After dessert Jay suggested that they all took their coffee in the large drawing room, and requested that Davina should bring it in to them. When he gave the order Todd glanced at Tanya while Pattie exchanged a tiny smile with her lover.

For Davina the evening had been rather boring. She couldn't imagine why Jay had felt it necessary to have her there. Clive could easily have waited on them all, and the cook had said that she hadn't requested any extra help. Placing the cups on the silver tray and pouring hot water into the coffee jug, Davina glanced at her watch. It was only ten-thirty. With any luck she'd be tucked up in bed at home in another half hour. She hoped that Jay was satisfied. The only possible explanation she could think of for his behaviour was that he'd hoped to annoy Phil. If that was the case he'd certainly succeeded.

The door of the drawing room had been left ajar,

making it easy for her to push it open with her shoulder, and as she concentrated on balancing everything she was only partly aware of what was going on in the room. It wasn't until she'd placed the tray on the mahogany coffee table and turned around that she fully realised what was happening.

Tanya was standing in the middle of the room. She'd removed her blouse and her upper torso was entirely naked except for a small gold chain hanging in a loop from her nipples. She was cupping her breasts with her hands and Davina could see that the nipples were red, fully engorged and the breasts looked swollen and tight. She swallowed hard. It was the first time she'd seen another woman in a state of sexual arousal and she didn't know how to react. Part of her wanted to run from the room, but another part didn't. She stood motionless as Jay crossed the floor and, reaching out, tugged lightly on the chain, causing Tanya to give a tiny squeal.

'What would you like me to do, honey?' he murmured seductively.

Tanya's almond-shaped eyes were bright with excitement and need. 'Lick my nipples,' she murmured. 'They feel so hot.'

Davina knew that she should go, that this was something she ought not to get involved in, but for some reason her legs wouldn't obey her brain and she remained rooted to the spot as Jay put his hands on his boss's wife's shoulders and bent his head until he was able to draw his tongue over the abused tip of Tanya's nipple.

The moment he did this Tanya began to whimper with pleasure and Todd, who was sitting in a chair opposite her, pulled Pattie onto his lap and started nuzzling her neck. 'I guess you'd like a little attention too,' he said and, grabbing his right hand, Pattie pulled it up to her left breast so that he could massage it through the silk material.

Davina couldn't believe her eyes. Never in her wildest dreams had she imagined anything like this. She wondered why Todd wasn't jealous, why he didn't mind that Jay was touching his wife so intimately, but it was obvious that the four of them had done this before. To her shame she found that she wished more than anything on earth that she'd been one of the guests at the dinner and that it was her, not Tanya, who was standing in the middle of the room with Jay licking at her nipples.

As Todd and Pattie started to caress each other, while at the same time shedding their clothes, Jay slowly removed Tanya's skirt. Davina saw that beneath it Todd's wife was totally naked except for a suspender belt and stockings. Her pubic hair was jet-black and Jay slid a hand down her body, his fingers parting the hair and then moving between her sex lips until he located her clitoris. Her hips jerked as she gasped with pleasure.

The moment he heard this Jay removed his hand and instead started tugging on the nipple chain until Tanya cried out with what Davina could tell was a mixture of pain and pleasure. 'Don't keep me waiting,' Todd's wife begged him. 'Not yet, let me have one quick orgasm first.'

'You beg so sweetly,' said Jay, but Davina, whose heart was thumping against her ribs, didn't believe that he was going to do as she asked. It seemed as though the four of them were totally oblivious to her. Now Jay pushed on Tanya's shoulders until she was sitting on the floor, then she lay down on her back with a moan of despair as she seemed to realise that despite her plea she was going to have to wait.

Davina glanced away from the couple for a moment to see what Pattie and Todd were doing. Pattie was kneeling facing the back of the chair, her arms folded along the top and her chin resting on her hands while Todd entered her from behind. He was moving his hands against her back so that her large breasts were constantly stimulated by the fabric of the chair. Clearly he wasn't making her wait as Jay was making Tanya wait. Pattie's cries became more and more urgent until, with a sudden scream of excitement, she climaxed and Davina watched the blonde girl's body trembling violently in the aftermath of release.

Jay was crouching over Tanya. He'd now removed the nipple chain and was rubbing the sore tip of her left nipple with his thumb. As he massaged it she uttered strange keening sounds of pleasure, sounds that made Davina's belly quake and she felt her juices start to flow. She knew that she had to get out of there, escape before she was lost, but she was hypnotised by all that she was seeing. Her excitement was so great that she wanted to stay because she was certain she'd be able to climax simply by watching the other four.

Jay grabbed Tanya's breast tightly in his hand and

then pulled it into his mouth, sucking so hard that she cried out in pain. He was clearly excited, his breathing ragged, and he lowered himself so that he could stimulate her clitoris with the head of his rigid erection.

Davina watched as Tanya's hips arched up off the floor. The Oriental girl was moaning with desire, balanced on the edge of release, desperate for a final caress that would topple her into fulfilment, but Jay refused to give her that final caress. When her breathing snagged in her throat he lifted his body off her so that she was no longer receiving stimulation where she most wanted it.

Davina's body ached almost as much as Tanya's appeared to, and she fully understood the young woman's despair. Todd and Pattie, momentarily relaxing, were watching with interest. 'How long are you gonna make her wait, Jay?' Todd called out.

'As long as I can,' gasped Jay, and Davina heard Tanya give a wail of frustration.

Now he was licking and sucking around Tanya's bellybutton, his teeth nibbling at the delicate flesh. She squealed with excited pleasure, her hips moving more and more frantically until finally he slid inside her, thrusting very slowly in and out, continuing to torment her until she started screaming at him, begging him to move faster, harder. Eventually, just when Davina wondered how Tanya could stand it, he pushed the prone girl's knees up against her shoulders, opening her wide for himself. He thrust in and out as their bodies moved together in what was obviously a well established rhythm.

Now Tanya's breathing grew more and more rapid. Her head thrashed from side to side on the carpet as her body gathered itself together for the blissful explosion that she'd been longing for. Davina felt her own muscles coiling and tightening and a pulse started to beat behind her clitoris. Incredulously she realised that she was about to come. As Tanya finally spasmed in ecstasy, Davina's whole body quaked and trembled as she took silent pleasure from the bittersweet contractions caused simply by watching the couple. She felt utterly ashamed of herself, yet at the same time she knew that she wouldn't have missed any of this for the world.

She wondered if the four Americans were so engrossed in what they were doing that they'd forgotten all about her. Certainly they took no notice of her, and she made a conscious effort to keep as still as possible. She was desperate not to draw attention to herself and perhaps be banished. However, as Jay sat down on the sofa, sprawling nude and totally unself-conscious over it, he stared directly across the room and his eyes were piercing as they travelled over her face. She waited for him to tell her to go, uncertain as to whether he would be angry or simply amused, but to her surprise he said nothing and after a few seconds looked away.

It was as though she didn't exist, as though it was of no importance to him whether she was there or not, but she knew that couldn't be true. He must want her there otherwise he would have ordered her to leave immediately. The knowledge that he knew she was there, was probably gaining pleasure from her presence, only increased her own excitement and she waited, wondering what would happen next.

As the men rested, Pattie moved a chair into the centre of the room then sat down on it and closed her eyes. Slowly Tanya began to spread perfumed oil over the blonde girl's body, her fingers skimming the flesh of the other woman's breasts, and Davina saw Pattie's nipples become instantly erect. Tanya's touch appeared to be feather-light and she skimmed her hands down the sides of the other woman's chest before massaging her belly with slow circular movements, her hands gliding easily over the oiled skin.

Soon Pattie was murmuring with contentment and Tanya took her by the hands and gently laid her on her side on the floor so that she could spread the oil over Pattie's back and buttocks. Pattie's eyes were still closed and her body was shaking with excitement as, with slow deliberation, Tanya allowed her nimble fingers to move between the girl's parted thighs. Now Pattie lay on her back, her knees apart, moaning with pleasure as Tanya parted her sex lips and allowed the oil to drip onto Pattie's opened vulva.

With each drop Davina instinctively flinched, her own hot damp flesh seeming to feel the cool liquid. Her clitoris swelled as once more her excitement grew and her flesh started to ache with thwarted need.

'That's gorgeous,' groaned Pattie. 'Don't stop now.'

Tanya's mouth curved upwards in a half smile, and bending her head she started to lick around the exposed clitoris, swirling her tongue in tiny delicate movements as Pattie started to groan and thrash on the carpet. It was obvious that she was about to come and Davina felt as though she herself would as well. She glanced at the two men and saw that both of them were already re-aroused. Jay's hips were twitching slightly as he watched his lover's pleasure start to spill.

When Pattie's body began to spasm Tanya slid two fingers inside her and Davina saw her thrusting them rapidly in and out. This appeared to drive Pattie out of her mind with pleasure and her whole body was racked with convulsions. Finally the spasms died away and Davina realised that this time she wasn't going to come. She was incredibly aroused, her panties damp with her own juices, her nipples hard and sticking out through her white blouse, but she needed a touch to trigger her orgasm and there was no one there to touch her.

At that moment Jay stood up and signalled for Todd to join him. It seemed that the two men were used to this because Todd immediately crouched on all fours, the muscles of his athletic body standing out clearly. Now Tanya leant backwards over him so that her body was arched like a bow, the soles of her feet firmly on the carpet. Jay knelt between her outspread legs and drew each of her nipples in turn into his mouth, sucking on them for several minutes. When he finally stopped Davina could see that both the nipples were bright red and she gasped as Jay promptly clipped the nipple chain back on to them and Tanya gave a whimper of surprise. Davina wondered how it must feel to have the swollen aching buds trapped in the tiny metal clips but from the way Tanya was squirming on her husband's back it looked as though she was enjoying herself.

Using his left hand Jay massaged Tanya's pubic mound and vulva, pressing hard with the heel of his hand over the area where the clitoris lay beneath the folded labia, and she gave a strangled gasp of rising pleasure. As his hand continued its remorseless titillation of her body he used his right hand to insert a vibrator inside Todd's wife.

'See if you can wait three minutes before you come,' he drawled.

Tanya uttered a desperate gurgling sound that Davina felt sure was a protest, but Pattie was now standing by them, a watch in her hand.

'I'll tell you when the time is up, Tanya,' she promised.

Davina could scarcely bear to watch. She could imagine so well how Tanya must feel as Jay cleverly manipulated her flesh, driving her wild with longing, but every time it looked as though she was about to come the pressure of his left hand would ease, or he would briefly remove the vibrator.

'Only thirty seconds to go,' said Pattie.

'Too long I guess,' murmured Jay, and as Davina watched he thrust the vibrator fiercely inside Tanya while at the same time pressing more firmly with his left hand. The Oriental girl gave a shriek of dismay as her pleasure spilt over and her body heaved on her husband's back.

'I guess you'll have to pay a forfeit,' said Jay, and there was amusement in his voice.

'Not straight away,' Tanya begged him, struggling to get up. 'I'm exhausted.'

'Surely not,' he remarked, helping her to her feet.

Suddenly Davina couldn't stand it any longer. She had to leave, had to get back to her cottage and give herself relief. It was obvious that the four of them were going to continue for some time, yet Davina knew she couldn't stay. She wanted to, wanted to see exactly how far they went, how depraved they were, but her screaming flesh needed a touch, some kind of stimulation to release her pent-up desire.

She started to move slowly towards the door and suddenly all four Americans turned to her. Tanya looked limp and exhausted but very content. Pattie's eyes were bright with excitement and she gave Davina a challenging stare, almost as though daring her to comment, while the two men simply watched her, their eyes assessing her reaction to what she'd witnessed.

She waited for them to speak, to say something, anything, but none of them did, and suddenly overwhelmed by embarrassment Davina fled. She rushed out of the main house, almost tripping on the gravel drive in her haste, not so much to get away from what she'd seen as to give herself the satisfaction that she needed so badly.

Chapter Seven

On the Monday morning Jay left Pattie sleeping off the excesses of the night before and walked swiftly across to Davina's cottage. He wondered how she'd greet him, and what she'd be expecting after the scenes she'd witnessed at the main house. He'd watched her very carefully the whole time that she'd been in the drawing room with them, and had been pleased to see from her reactions that he was right about her. Although clearly shocked she'd been unable to leave, and her swift arousal had been encouraging.

It was a long time since Jay had felt quite so exhilarated by the chase as he was now, and he silently thanked his godfather for giving him this opportunity. At the same time, he couldn't help wondering exactly what had been in David's mind. He'd had no illusions about Jay, they'd frequently discussed the younger man's private life, and although Jay had never gone into details he knew that David had understood the principles by which he lived.

It seemed strange that he should word his will in such a way that his niece should be at the mercy of Jay's desires, but Jay suspected that had David lived longer the will would have been changed. It may well have been his way of hoping that, should anything happen to him earlier, Davina would be forced to realise that she was wasting herself, that she should live life to the full while she was young.

Davina opened the door to him but she wasn't able to look him in the eye. 'You're prompt,' she said quietly.

'Yeah, I've gotta go to London this afternoon and wanted to get everything straight before I left.'

'You've only just got *back* from London.'

'Sure, this is just a dinner date. Mind if I come in?' Even as he asked the question he saw a look of relief in her eyes and knew that she'd been anticipating such a request, doubtless waiting eagerly to see what he was going to do. Well, she was in for quite a surprise.

She glanced briefly at him. 'You haven't brought any clothes for me,' she said flatly.

Jay shook his head. 'I'm not stopping.' He waited silently, watching her as carefully as he'd watch a witness in the stand, gauging her reaction and not speaking until the silence grew awkward. This was something he liked to do, it put the opponent at a disadvantage. Although Davina wasn't exactly an opponent she was rapidly becoming a quarry, albeit a very beautiful and desirable one. 'Aren't you going to ask why?' he continued.

He was amused to see how hard she tried to look disinterested. 'It's none of my business.'

'In this case it is. I want you to act as my companion for the evening.'

'What about Pattie?'

'She isn't suitable. I'm dining with Brits and they always assume that leggy blondes are dumb. I can't have them thinking I've got a dumb girlfriend, can I?'

'What time will we be back?' she asked nervously.

'We'll come back tomorrow. I won't be able to drive tonight, not if I'm going to drink.'

'Where would I stay?'

'I'll book us a couple of rooms in a nearby hotel.'

Davina hesitated. 'I suppose that will be all right then,' she conceded, but Jay sensed she was more disappointed than relieved.

'I'll pick you up at six-thirty. We're eating at eight-thirty which gives us plenty of time to check in to our hotel, get changed and have a drink before we all meet up.'

'What kind of thing should I wear?' Davina asked.

'Gee, don't ask me. I haven't a clue about women's clothes. I'm better on underwear.'

'What I meant was, is it very formal?'

'No, but smart. Sophisticated yet slightly sexy is the look you'd better aim for. How's the work going?' he added as an afterthought.

'I've finished the sci-fi. I posted it on Saturday. My next commission's for a book of children's fairy stories.'

'Quite a change.'

'More my style,' she said demurely.

Jay shook his head. 'I don't think so, honey. I saw

you last night. I was watching you and you enjoyed it all. It turned you on. Come on, admit it.'

'I don't want to talk about it.' Her tone was defensive and Jay decided not to pursue the matter.

'Suit yourself. I'll see you this evening. Make sure you're ready, won't you?'

'Don't worry, I won't let you down. I presume this is my rent payment for the week?'

'Sure, the first half at least.'

When he picked her up that evening Davina was clearly ill at ease. She placed a case containing her dress in the boot before getting into the passenger seat, her long legs slanted sideways. 'Anything wrong?' asked Jay.

'I don't really think I should be doing this,' muttered Davina.

'Why the hell not? If it's Phil you're worried about I'd have thought he'd consider you sitting around in front of me in your underwear far worse.'

'I wasn't thinking about Phil.'

'Can't you ever relax and enjoy yourself?'

'You're not a very relaxing person to be with,' she retorted.

Jay nodded. 'I guess that's true. This is a social evening though so we'd better try and have a good time.'

Despite what he'd said he made no great effort to keep the conversation flowing, preferring to let silence spark off an erotic charge between them. When they arrived at the hotel he saw her eyes widen in surprise. 'Is this it? I thought we'd be staying at the Savoy or somewhere like that.'

'Sorry to disappoint you, honey. Believe me, it's better than it looks from the outside,' he added, realising that the plain terraced house in the quiet London side street must look very disappointing if she'd been expecting the glitz and glamour of a large hotel. 'This place is pretty exclusive. My father used to stay here, and so did your Uncle David. I don't suppose either of them stayed here alone either.'

Davina's head turned sharply towards him. 'You don't know anything about what Uncle David did in London. Don't you think it's pretty despicable to try and make him sound like you?'

'You think I'm despicable then?'

'Yes,' she said defiantly. 'After what I saw last night, I do.'

'Then why didn't you say so at the time?'

'It wasn't my place.'

'You could have left.'

'I know,' her voice was so low that he could hardly catch her words. 'I should have gone, but ... '

'It's okay,' he assured her. 'I know exactly why you stayed. Come on, let's find our rooms and get changed.'

Once inside the front door they were discreetly welcomed by a middle-aged woman who Jay had met a couple of times before on his visits. He saw Davina glancing around in amazement, her eyes taking in the plush surroundings.

'This place has four storeys,' he explained. 'All the rooms are en-suite, and discretion and privacy are assured. It's really a kinda club I guess.'

'But not for gentlemen,' exclaimed Davina.

Jay couldn't help laughing. 'Maybe you're right. It depends on your definition of a gentleman. Do you think Phil's a gentleman?'

Her response was swift. 'I don't want to talk about Phil.'

'I don't blame you. He's the most boring subject in the world. Even the weather's more interesting than Phil.'

'I don't think Pattie feels like that about him.'

Jay's eyes narrowed. 'Why do you say that?'

She shrugged. 'It's just a feeling I've got.'

Jay felt relieved. At least she didn't know for certain. As he drew her inexorably into his strange world he wanted to know that she was following willingly, not as a form of revenge on Phil for his fling with Pattie.

At eight o'clock precisely, Davina walked into the small bar of the hotel and Jay noticed every man's head turn. She was wearing a claret-coloured velvet dress that clung to her slender but shapely body. It had an elegant cowl neck and a plunging back that reached down to her waist, leaving the creamy skin and the delicate bones of her spine totally exposed. She was wearing tiny pearl stud earrings and had a pearl bracelet around her right wrist, while on her left wrist a gold and diamond watch glittered. Her stockings had a soft silky sheen to them, and her shoes were black with high heels and a tiny ankle strap.

Jay felt a terrible desire not to go out to dinner. Instead he wanted to rush her upstairs and ravish her unmercifully on his bed, but he knew that the satisfaction would only be fleeting. It was far better to play the game the way he'd planned, to make them both wait.

'Very nice,' he said smoothly. 'Would you like a drink before we leave?'

Davina shook her head. 'I think we ought to be going. You don't want to be late, do you?' He could hear the mockery in her voice.

'I sure as hell don't. Okay, let's go.'

The dinner went exactly as he'd planned. They were dining with one of the country's leading barristers and his wife, and Davina made just the sort of impression Jay had hoped. He noticed that despite the fact that he'd always considered her quite shy, she made conversation easily and he could tell that Christopher Parkinson was impressed. Confident of Davina's ability to handle things, when not discussing points of law Jay was able to focus his attention on Christopher's wife, Lizzie, who was a legal secretary at Lincoln's Inn and fascinated by the differences in the British and American legal systems.

'Don't you think it strange how far apart the systems have drifted considering that yours was originally based on ours?' she asked Jay towards the end of the evening.

'Nope. The truth is, it's your system that's changed.

It's become weaker, more obsessed with social workers and the rights of criminals. In my country we still put the victims first.'

'That's probably because there are so many of them,' remarked Christopher.

Jay shook his head. 'Did you know that a recent survey showed you were more likely to be mugged in England than in America?'

'I don't believe it,' said Lizzie.

'It's true,' Davina chipped in. 'I read that too. Mind you, people can make figures say anything they want.'

'None of you want to believe it, that's all,' said Jay. 'You like the horror stories about madmen running amok with guns in my country. I guess it makes you feel superior.'

'That's very rude,' said Davina, and Jay looked at her in surprise. 'You sound as though you've got a chip on your shoulder,' she said.

'I promise you I haven't,' he replied, attempting a smile although inside he was less than pleased.

'She's got you there,' said Christopher, patting Davina on the arm with what Jay considered unnecessary familiarity. 'Would you care to dance, my dear?'

the older man continued, and Jay watched as Davina and Christopher took to the floor.

'I don't dance,' said Lizzie, 'so don't feel that you have to ask me.'

'That's a pity, I'd have enjoyed taking you on the floor,' said Jay casually.

Lizzie leant closer to him. 'I'd have enjoyed it too,' she said softly, and he realised that if he wanted her she was available. Not now of course, that would be impossible, but at a later date.

'You have my husband's telephone number, don't you?' she continued. Jay nodded. 'Good. You must let us know next time you're in town. Of course my husband may be busy, but I'd be more than happy to show you around.'

'You're very kind,' said Jay. 'I enjoy seeing new sights.'

At that moment Christopher and Davina returned to the table and immediately Jay got to his feet. 'My turn now.'

He led her out onto the dance floor and was pleased when the music slowed. He always enjoyed dancing with tall women, it was so much more comfortable and her chin rested neatly on his shoulder. His right arm was around her waist, his left hand resting lightly on her shoulder as he steered her carefully between the other dancers.

He pulled her a little closer to him so that their bodies were joined. 'Do you know what I'd like to do to you tonight?' he murmured in her ear. 'I want to take you back to the hotel and undress you slowly. I want to lick every inch of your gorgeous body. I'd like to hear you whimpering with desire, to see you arching your hips towards me, hear you begging me to enter you.' He could feel her trembling against him but she kept her head buried against his jacket and didn't reply. 'Wouldn't you like that too?' he asked, allowing the fingers of his left hand to caress the top of her bare arm. 'Imagine how it would feel if I was touching you like this elsewhere. On the soft skin at the top of your inner thighs, or here.'

As he spoke he moved his left hand until he was drawing tiny circles on her bare back. He used the soft pads of his fingers and heard her draw in her breath sharply while at the same time her hips pressed instinctively closer to his and he knew that she must be feeling the hardness of his erection.

When the dance finally ended and they sat down opposite each other again her face was flushed. Although she wouldn't look at him, her eyes were shining. Christopher looked knowingly at Jay while Lizzie's mouth set in a tight line.

Seated at a table on the far side of the room, Phil Burnett had watched the couple incredulously, his face red with fury. He'd felt like getting up, crossing the floor and hitting Jay Prescott hard on the jaw, before dragging Davina out of the restaurant. Unfortunately for him, he was about to close a lucrative sale with his two dining companions. If he blew it, he'd almost certainly lose his job and so he kept silent. However, the rage ate into him, ruining both the meal and the anticipated pleasure of the business deal.

Half an hour later Christopher got to his feet. 'Time we were going, Lizzie. It was a great evening, Jay. You've got those names and addresses that I gave you?' Jay nodded. 'Make sure you contact them all. Every one of them is known personally to me and they'll be extremely helpful. Jeffrey might want to come over to America on a reciprocal visit some time, so he'll probably be particularly amenable.'

'Thanks a lot, you've been a great help,' said Jay, clasping the older man's hand firmly in his. Then he turned to Lizzie. As he kissed her on the cheek he touched the side of her neck softly with his right hand in a tiny intimate gesture that he knew would please her. It wasn't that he necessarily thought he'd take her up on her offer, but it was always possible that she'd provide an interesting break for him at some time.

'Enjoy the evening?' he asked Davina as he hailed a cab to take them back to their hotel.

'It was very nice,' she said politely, rather like a little girl who'd been to a party. 'I hope I did everything right.'

'You were perfect,' he assured her. 'The question is, will you do everything right later tonight?' Before she could answer they were getting into the cab and Jay settled back against the seat, looking forward to the next few hours with keen anticipation.

Back at the hotel the pair of them entered the lift in silence, and neither spoke until they reached the door to Davina's room. She hesitated, uncertain as to what she should do now. She'd never felt like this before. Her skin was tingling and she still seemed able to feel the touch of his fingers on her back, where he'd caressed her as they danced together. She was highly aroused and certain that he knew it, yet despite this she knew that it was up to him to make a move. He wasn't the kind of man who would expect her to suggest that she joined him, and in any case she wasn't certain that she'd be able to utter the words.

'Perhaps you'd care for a drink before you retire?' suggested Jay.

His expression was perfectly neutral. She tried to read it, tried to tell whether he was as excited as she was, but it was impossible. He was wearing the bland mask of the lawyer and as usual had his feelings well under control. 'That sounds like a good idea,' she said after a slight pause, anxious not to sound too eager.

A few minutes later he was handing her a glass of brandy and she sat down in one of the large armchairs, trying hard not to look at the huge bed that dominated the room. Jay, glass in hand, walked around the room and she could tell that he was as restless as she was. 'Do you remember what I said to you when we were dancing?' he asked abruptly, turning to face her.

Davina nodded. 'It was all true. I still want to do those things.'

Davina shivered. 'I'd like you to do them.'

His expression softened and he took the glass from her, then, drawing her to her feet and reaching behind her, he slowly unfastened the zip of her dress while at the same time his lips brushed against her ear.

Once the dress was off he sat her on the foot of the bed and removed each of her shoes in turn before taking off her right stocking. His hands caressed every inch of her leg, and when the stocking was finally off he lifted her leg into the air and gently nibbled at her toes before repeating the whole exercise again on the other leg.

She was trembling violently now, almost hypnotised by this slow, gentle seduction that was such a contrast to his powerful physical appearance and naturally dominating manner. The contrast only added to the erotic thrill, and when he finally unclipped her bra and eased her panties down before lying her back on the bed she felt as though she'd come at any second.

'Spread your legs apart a little,' he murmured, lying down beside her and propping himself up on one elbow as his eyes lingered on her body. Then, finally, he started to slowly caress her from top to toe, his left hand moving with exquisite lightness over her breasts, belly and thighs until she began to squirm restlessly as the blood coursed through her veins. She felt her clitoris hardening as her sex lips parted in readiness for the touch that her body so urgently needed.

Only then, when she was half out of her mind with need, did he begin to touch her between her thighs, allowing his finger to trail along the moist flesh, massaging her own juices into her and occasionally brushing against the side of her clitoris. Every time he did this her hips jerked and her breathing snagged. She heard herself start to whimper and his eyes softened.

'Not much longer,' he murmured. 'I want to make this good for you.'

He already was. No one had ever made love to her like this before, and although she was desperately in need of release she also wanted the foreplay to go on forever. He moved down the bed and carefully eased a finger inside her, pressing upwards until he touched a spot that was new to her and she felt a delicious heat begin to spread through the whole of her pubic area.

Maintaining the pressure he lowered his head and at last his tongue circled her aching clitoris. The moment it did so she spasmed helplessly in an ecstasy of pleasure as the glorious contractions pulsated through her.

As she climaxed she was aware that he was watching her, and he looked pleased, as though he was taking pleasure from her pleasure. When the last tiny spasms died away she started to sit up but he gently pushed her back again. 'Keep still,' he whispered. 'You can leave it all to me tonight.'

She was aware that he was parting her sex lips, opening her up to him and for a moment she felt ridiculously shy but then she gasped as he eased the head of a vibrator inside her. 'Relax,' he urged her. 'Give yourself over to the pleasure.' His words reassured her and she closed her eyes as the pulsations from the vibrator started to arouse all her nerve endings, sending jagged flames of pleasure scorching through her body. She'd never been as excited before and now she was crying out, terrified that the ultimate pleasure would elude her. 'Trust me,' he reminded her. His free hand wandered over her belly and then caressed the slender curve of her waist, while all the time the vibrator continued to stimulate her until once more her body trembled as her pleasure spilled.

Jay lay beside her, pulling her onto her side so that they were facing each other and his hands gripped her hips as he lifted her outer leg over his top thigh. She stared deep into his eyes as he carefully eased the tip of his erection inside her. He was far larger than Phil, larger even than her husband had been. For a moment she tensed against the invasion but his mouth closed over hers and his tongue flicked around the inside of her lips and against her gums. As she responded her whole body softened and he was able to thrust fully inside her. It felt incredible. She was so lubricated from all that had gone before that the glorious hot pulsations quickly started again as he moved rhythmically in and out of her. Then, to her astonishment, he reached behind, parted the cheeks of her bottom and started to ease a finger inside her rectum.

'No!' she cried, trying to twist away from him.

'Keep still,' he urged her. 'It will feel good, I promise. Just breathe through your mouth for a few seconds, let your muscles get used to it. You'll have your best climax ever.'

Davina wanted to refuse, but as soon as she did as he suggested she felt an extraordinary excitement build deep within her as incredibly sensitive nerve endings, endings that had never been touched before, were stimulated by his forbidden caress.

She felt as though she were going out of her mind. He was moving hard inside her now, and at the same time moving the finger, tapping lightly against the walls of her forbidden entrance. The combination of sensations was shattering. She squirmed, helpless in this new-found world of sensuality and her nipples rubbed against his hard, muscular chest. She felt the tension within her building rapidly, fast approaching the point of no return and her body began to arch into a bow so that Jay had to pull her against him. 'That's it, honey,' he murmured against her mouth. 'This is the big one.'

His words drove her over-stimulated body to fever pitch and with a scream of delight she climaxed once more, and this time the pleasure was so intense that it felt as though it was going to tear her apart. She was still whimpering as the delicious final flickers travelled through her when Jay's climax came. She felt him pumping inside her, spilling himself deep within her, groaning loudly and shuddering from head to foot.

For a few minutes they remained closely entwined and Davina could tell that he, like her, was surprised by the intensity of his orgasm. He looked confused now, as though this wasn't what he'd expected. To her surprise he gripped her head with his hands and kissed her savagely for several minutes before sliding out of her and moving onto his back. She lay quietly. Her body felt so light that she was surprised she wasn't floating and she was just about to tell him how wonderful it had been when he spoke. 'You sure as hell must value that cottage. You pulled out all the stops for me tonight, didn't you?'

She was stunned. He'd seemed so tender, so caring, that the words were like a slap in the face. She'd felt safe with him, certain that there was more than just sex involved, and she wondered how she could have been such a fool. Not that she regretted it, it was still the best sex she'd ever had, but his words had changed everything.

'I like to pay for everything in full,' she said calmly, determined that he would never know how much he'd hurt her. 'I wouldn't want you to feel that I wasn't paying you the full amount.'

'Nope, I reckon that was about fair,' he said agreeably. 'Guess you'd better get back to your own room now. Unless you want to pay for the whole week in one night?'

Davina suddenly felt horribly aware of the fact that she was naked and her skin had turned cold. 'No, I don't think so.'

'I didn't think you would. You enjoyed it though, didn't you?'

She was trying desperately to dress herself but the clothes were far more reluctant to go on than they had been to come off. 'Of course I did. You're very expert.'

'Is there something wrong?' he demanded.

Davina shook her head. 'What could be wrong?'

'Search me. You know, Todd would enjoy watching you. Come to that, Todd would enjoy taking you. Do you like Todd?'

Davina's mouth went dry. 'I like him as a person,' she said carefully.

Jay laughed. 'You know damn well that's not what I meant. Never mind, we can talk about it another time. I'm tired. Sleep well, Davina.'

Back in her room Davina quickly undressed, show-ered and got into bed. She still didn't understand what had happened. On reflection she was certain that she hadn't been wrong. Jay had cared at the beginning, and even afterwards, but then everything had changed and she didn't understand why. The only thing that she could think of was that he'd expected her to refuse him at some stage, and that by going along with everything she'd disappointed him. Not physically, clearly in that direction she'd been more than satisfactory, but if he was wanting to get her out of the cottage then he must be feeling very disappointed.

'I'm not going to be that easy to get rid of, Jay Prescott,' she murmured. 'No matter what you ask of me, I'll do it. It's my cottage. You'll be back in America in a year's time but I'll still be in Oxford no matter how hard you try to get rid of me.'

It was only in the last seconds before she fell asleep that Davina realised exactly what this might cost her. After tonight there was no knowing what price Jay would demand in lieu of rent, and that this might be why he'd been so anxious for her to witness him and his friends as they indulged in group sex. Even so, if that was what she had to do then she'd do it. He might be stubborn and used to getting what he wanted but in a different way she knew that she could be stubborn too, especially where her home was concerned.

Chapter Eight

Pattie drew back the bedroom curtains and as she stared out blearily across the garden she saw that it was going to be another scorching day. She felt exhausted. She, Todd and Tanya had enjoyed a very energetic evening the previous night and today her muscles ached slightly, but she smiled at the memory of her pleasure. Then a frown creased her forehead. It would have been even more pleasurable had Jay been there. Unfortunately Jay had decided to stay overnight in London with Davina, and despite his assurances that nothing would happen between them Pattie wasn't convinced.

Although she thought it unlikely that they'd have

had sex she was certain Jay would have taken the opportunity to exert some kind of spell over the English girl in order for her to be willing to participate in one of his sexual games, and she wasn't certain that she entirely approved. At that moment the telephone began to ring and she picked up the receiver beside the bed. 'Hello?'

'Is that Pattie?' asked a male voice. After a few seconds' delay she placed it as belonging to Phil Burnett.

'Sure is, or was when I last looked in the mirror.'

'I saw Jay and Davina dancing together in London last night,' he blurted out.

'He took her to a business dinner. Guess I was too American, seeing as how he was dining with Brits. He kinda thought Davina would make a better impression.'

'She was certainly making a good impression on him,' said Phil angrily. 'They were dancing so closely you'd have thought they were stuck together with Superglue.'

Pattie's hand gripped the receiver tightly. 'Where was this?'

'The Place, I don't know if you know it but . . .'

'Yeah, I know it. He told me they were eating there. It's the new "in" restaurant.'

'Are they back yet? I've been trying to ring Davina at the cottage but there's no answer.'

'That's because they're still in London,' explained Pattie. 'Jay likes a drink or two when he's entertaining. He'd never risk drinking and driving.'

'But Davina can drive.'

'Seems like she drank too.'

'Don't you care?' shouted Phil, and Pattie moved the receiver slightly away from her ear. 'You would if you'd seen them.'

'Gee, it was just Jay being friendly. He's heard that Englishmen like to get on with their tenants.'

'Well, it might not trouble you but it infuriates me,' said Phil.

Secretly Pattie was livid. She'd never for one moment imagined the pair of them dancing intimately together, particularly since she knew that with Jay this was usually a prelude to sex. Her mind raced as she tried to think how best to deal with the situation. 'Well, you know what they say, don't get mad get even.'

'What does that mean?' Phil's tone was surly.

'Exactly what it says. We're having a little party here on Saturday. Davina isn't involved. It's just a few of our friends who are in England for a week or so and they're coming here for the Saturday night, so the wine will flow, if you get my meaning. Why don't you and Davina come too?'

'How can we if Jay doesn't invite us?'

'I'll tell him I invited you,' said Pattie. 'I am the hostess.'

'What difference will that make?'

'You can confront Jay about what you saw,' suggested Pattie.

'He's not likely to tell me what happened, is he?'

'Maybe not, but I don't think you should get too worried. Davina looks a faithful kind of girl to me. Don't forget, Phil, you've already had some fun with me. If anything has happened you can hardly complain, and nor can I.'

'She's changed since he arrived,' muttered Phil.

Pattie felt a chill run through her. This wasn't good news. 'Well, you can always dance with me the way you saw him dancing with Davina,' she suggested.

'Would you like that?' Suddenly Phil sounded more cheerful.

Legacy of Desire

'Honey, I'd adore it,' murmured Pattie huskily. 'You were just great on the summerhouse steps. I've been thinking about it ever since.' It was a complete lie; until that moment she'd totally forgotten it since its prime purpose, to make Jay jealous, had failed, but right now it seemed the best thing to say.

'Okay then, we'll come,' agreed Phil enthusiastically.

Pattie replaced the receiver and sat on the edge of the large bed. It'd been bad enough sleeping there alone. Despite all that had gone on between her, Todd and Tanya she'd still missed Jay. As soon as she'd woken she'd rolled over, reaching automatically for his morning erection. He often started the day with sex and although it wasn't a long drawn out session he made certain she was satisfied before it finished. She hoped that he hadn't reached for Davina this morning instead of her.

There was a light tap on the door. 'May I come in?' asked Tanya.

'Sure.'

'It's a great day, we could ...' Tanya's voice trailed off. 'You look sorta low. Something wrong? I thought we had a great time last night.'

Pattie told her about the telephone call and Tanya looked thoughtful. 'What did you do?'

'Invited Phil and Davina to the party on Saturday.'

Tanya pulled a face. 'Do you think that's wise?'

'What the hell else can I do?'

'Maybe you're playing right into his hands,' said Tanya.

'If he cares for me at all he'll show his jealousy eventually,' said Pattie firmly. 'Let's ask Todd what he thinks.'

They found Todd in the study and had to wait nearly half an hour before he got off the phone. 'It looks as though Jay might be needed back in Boston soon,' he remarked. 'Not for long, a couple of weeks or so.'

'I thought he was over here on a sabbatical,' said Pattie. 'How come you're not called back? You're his boss.'

'That's why I've decided he should go. I'm enjoying myself too much. Besides, I'm on vacation.'

'It might be the best thing,' Tanya murmured to Pattie.

'How come?' enquired Todd.

Tanya explained about Phil's phone call and what

Pattie had done. 'Do you think she's done the right thing?' she asked her husband.

Todd looked thoughtful. 'I guess you can never be certain with Jay, but on balance I'd say no. You ain't gonna make a man jealous who isn't capable of jealousy, Pattie.'

'Everyone's capable of jealousy if they care enough,' she retorted.

'Do you really want to know if he *doesn't* care enough?'

'What are you trying to say?'

'I'm not trying to say anything but I probably know Jay better than anyone, and I don't think that in all his thirty years he's yet met a woman capable of making him jealous.'

'But he's met women he cares about?' Pattie was beginning to feel frightened.

'I suppose, for a time, but it never lasts.'

'It's lasted with us.'

'Sure, longer than with anyone else but maybe the sand's running through the hour-glass a little bit quicker than you realise. If it is there's nothing you can do about it, Pattie. If you start trying to push him in a direction he doesn't want to go he'll get real stubborn.'

'He's real stubborn all the time. I won't know the difference.'

'You will when he suggests you pack your bags,' said Todd, and with that he walked out of the room.

Tanya looked uncomfortable. 'Todd can be a bit blunt sometimes,' she said quietly. 'I guess the call from America must have rattled him. Something's gone wrong at work and he hates that.'

'He doesn't think Jay's going to marry me, does he?'

'I've never asked him.'

Pattie took all her courage in both hands. 'Do you think he's going to marry me, Tanya?'

'Honestly?' Pattie nodded. 'Then I guess I've gotta say no. I don't think he's going to get married for another ten years or so. He's more interested in his work, and sexual variety.'

'But surely it would do his career good if he married?'

'It doesn't do him any harm being known as one of Boston's most eligible bachelors. He gets asked to a lot of dinners because of that. You'd be surprised how many mothers want him for their daughters.'

'Well, they're gonna be unlucky,' said Pattie fiercely. 'Sexually we suit each other perfectly, he's always saying that. Where's he going to find anyone better?'

'For sex possibly nowhere, but the day Jay starts to think about marriage he's going to consider more than that.'

'Like what?' asked Pattie aggressively. She had a suspicion that neither Todd nor Tanya felt she was good enough for Jay.

'Like family background and education, I suppose.'

'It didn't seem to trouble Todd when he married you,' snapped Pattie and then, when she saw the hurt on Tanya's face, she wished she'd kept quiet. 'I didn't mean that,' she said hastily. 'It's just that I really care for Jay and ...'

'But you don't love him,' said Tanya softly. 'You love the sex, and you want the position in Bostonian society that he can give you but you don't really love him. Think about it, Pattie. Maybe it isn't just a case of you not being right for him. Maybe he's not the right guy for you.'

'He is,' insisted Pattie, feeling almost sick with anger, 'and I'm going to make sure he realises it.'

*

In London, as Jay and Davina were driving back to Oxford, Phil was on a high. Already he was imagining the party on Saturday night and what he and Pattie might do together. When he'd rung her to tell her that he'd seen Jay and Davina he'd never for one moment imagined her inviting him to a private party. He'd simply wanted to make her feel as bad as he did, but this was even better. She was gorgeous, the sort of woman he'd often dreamt of but never imagined meeting. Of course the fact that she was Jay's mistress was a bit of a drawback, but he knew that Americans liked the kudos of British partners, and also knew that she'd enjoyed their sex together.

As he showed people round expensive properties and negotiated mortgages over the phone, he kept picturing Pattie's naked body, the perfectly sculpted breasts, the tanned skin and the trim waist and tight high buttocks. She was a little more rounded than Davina but every muscle was taut. She was physical perfection and simply thinking about her was enough to keep him in a state of perpetual arousal.

He supposed that he ought to feel guilty about Davina, and told himself that he would have done if it hadn't been for the fact that he'd seen her snuggling up to Jay Prescott, dancing with him in a way she'd never danced with Phil. 'Two can play at that game,' he muttered.

'Sorry?' Craig, working at the desk opposite his, looked at him questioningly.

'Nothing,' said Phil hastily. 'Just thinking aloud.'

'Quite nice thoughts by the look on your face.'

'Very nice thoughts,' Phil confirmed.

As he drove back to his flat that night he realised that he was looking forward to his forthcoming Oxfordshire visit more than he'd looked forward to one for a long time. Lately Davina had seemed different, as though she expected more from him, but he didn't know in what way. It wasn't as though she was like Pattie, the type of girl who you could tumble out of doors. Davina was far too shy and self-contained for anything like that. She was even quiet at the height of passion, whereas Pattie had been noisy the whole time, which in itself had been a turn-on. 'Roll on Friday,' he said cheerfully. It seemed that spotting Jay and Davina together hadn't been such a disaster after all.

*

'What did Jay say when Pattie told him she'd invited Phil and Davina to the party tonight?' Tanya asked her husband as he zipped up the black silk shift dress that was covered with hand-sewn sequins and ended just above her knee with a scalloped three-tier hemline edged with a row of tiny beads.

'According to Pattie he didn't show any reaction. I wasn't surprised, like I said, this kinda game won't work with Jay.'

Tanya nodded. 'I agree. I think Davina's sweet. If only Jay were more willing to commit himself I'd say they'd make the perfect couple. Boston would love her.'

'But would she love Boston?' queried Todd.

'I think so. I wonder if we could help the romance along a little?'

Todd kissed the nape of his wife's neck and ran his fingers through her sleek black bob. 'Why is it that you women always want to interfere?'

'I think Jay's going to miss a golden opportunity if he treats Davina the way he's treated his other women. He's keen on her, we both know that, Todd. The thing is, how can we help him overcome his aversion to commitment?'

'No, the thing is, how can I get you to keep your nose out of his affairs?' teased Todd.

'We could help,' persisted Tanya. 'Why don't you pay Davina some attention tonight? I'll see how Jay reacts and we'll take it from there. If he cares like I think he does he won't be able to stop himself from showing it, even if it's just for a minute or two.'

'It's a big party tonight,' said Todd patiently. 'Jay probably won't notice if I start flirting with Davina. Besides, you know what he's like. He'd say I was free to do what I liked.'

'What he says and what he feels are two completely different things.'

'Okay!' Todd threw up his hands in mock resignation. 'It's a good job I never had to cross-examine you in court, I'd have ended up the loser. Why is it I can never say no to you?'

Tanya wrapped her arms round his neck and kissed him full on the mouth. 'Because you love me?'

'Guess that must be it.'

'Right, then let's go and join the party,' said Tanya triumphantly.

By nine o'clock the house was full. Between them Jay

and Pattie had invited far more people than Todd had expected, and lots of them were strangers to him. It took him a while to find Davina, but eventually he saw Pattie standing talking to Phil in an animated fashion and moved over towards her, guessing that Davina wouldn't be far away.

Pattie had swept her hair over to the right-hand side of her head, letting it fall in front of her shoulder and leaving her left ear exposed. Her make-up was immaculate and she was wearing one enormous diamond earring in her left ear, a gift from Jay as Todd remembered. She was wearing a stunning, column-shaped sleeveless navy jersey dress and her full breasts were accentuated by a gold buckled belt that she wore tightly cinched round her waist. She was wearing no other jewellery apart from the earring but she didn't need any; her blonde beauty stood out. Even Todd, who wasn't that keen on blondes, had to admit that she looked incredible.

'Hey! Talk about dressed to kill,' he said with a smile, moving in on her and Phil as the pair of them stood almost touching, Davina standing awkwardly on Phil's left. 'Hi, Davina,' he added. 'Great to see you again, honey. Love the top.'

Davina, who was wearing an embroidered magenta velvet top with a button-through front and cut-away hem over a long black skirt with a side split to the knee, smiled half-heartedly. 'I'm not sure I'm glamorous enough,' she murmured.

'I like the understated English look,' he assured her, taking her by the elbow and steering her away from the other two towards the drinks. 'What can I get you, sweetie?'

'White wine will be fine.'

As Todd handed her a drink he inhaled her perfume, a light floral fragrance far less cloying than those favoured by Pattie or Tanya, and he thought how fresh and unspoilt she seemed. He was also attracted by her coolness, mixed with an enchanting vulnerability he hadn't seen in a woman for a very long time. 'Been here long?'

'About fifteen minutes. I didn't want to come, but Phil said Pattie had invited us so I thought ...'

'You thought it best to stay on the right side of her, yeah?'

Davina nodded and her fingers fiddled restlessly with the stem of the wine glass. 'To be honest I was surprised. I didn't think Pattie was very keen on me, but now we're here I can see that's not the reason we were invited.'

'You mean she's coming on to Phil?' Davina nodded. 'Hell, that's nothing. Pattie does that automatically. Why don't you and I have a dance?'

She smiled. 'That would be nice, Todd.' He realised that he was becoming aroused, and as they started to move together on the dance floor he knew that she must be aware of this. Her dark eyes widened slightly but apart from that she gave no responding signal. When the music stopped he led her out of the drawing room, down the hall and into the billiard room which was empty. She looked around hesitantly, clearly nervous about the fact that they were alone together.

'Hey, come on. What do you think I'm gonna do?' Todd said.

Davina shrugged. 'I'm sorry. I was just wondering where Phil and Pattie were.'

'Back in the other room, weren't they?'

'No, I saw them leave while we were dancing.'

'Is that a fact? Maybe they've gone out to get some air.'

'Maybe.' She didn't sound as though she believed him.

'Let's not worry about them,' he suggested, leaning against the billiard table and lightly stroking Davina's left arm with his right hand. 'You're a classy dame, but I'm sure you know that.'

Davina looked even more uncomfortable. 'Englishmen don't pay compliments like you Americans,' she murmured. 'I don't quite know how to answer you.'

Out of the corner of his eye Todd saw Pattie and Phil coming into the room. Phil had his arm round Pattie's waist and the pair of them were kissing and caressing each other, both clearly highly excited.

'Then don't answer me,' he said to Davina. Before she had a chance to protest he put his hands either side of her waist, lifted her onto the billiard table then stood between her legs, his hands resting on the polished surface each side of her body. He wanted to start caressing her, not because Tanya had suggested it but because he was attracted to her, and the knowledge that Phil was in the room only increased this attraction.

Running his hands up and down the sides of her body he bent his head and kissed the skin at the base of her throat, where the delicate bones were visible. She let her head fall back a little but as she did so she caught sight of Phil and immediately sat bolt upright.

Todd realised that Phil, who had now sat down in one of the chairs and was busy pulling Pattie onto his lap, hadn't noticed it was Davina on the table. Davina watched, mortified, as her boyfriend started to struggle with Pattie's clothing, his urgency only too clear. Pattie was laughing with excitement. As she pulled off Phil's shirt and tie she allowed her blonde hair to brush across his chest and he uttered a soft throaty sound of pleasure.

'Get me out of here,' Davina whispered urgently to Todd.

Reluctantly he helped her off the table and the pair of them slipped out of the room, but when Davina made to go back to the main room Todd gripped her tightly by the wrist and led her firmly towards the stairs. 'We'll go somewhere private,' he promised her. 'Look, honey, your boyfriend feels free to have a good time. Why don't you and I do the same?'

'But I'm not in love with you,' she exclaimed.

Todd laughed. 'Hell, I'd have rather a shock if you

were. You don't have to be in love with me to let me give you pleasure. You saw us all the other night, you know how the game's played.'

'But I need to feel something for you, otherwise it won't work.'

'Give it a try,' Todd urged her. 'Wouldn't you like to enjoy yourself for an hour?'

He watched her struggle with herself and then, probably remembering Phil, she nodded. 'All right,' she agreed and he felt a surge of triumph as they sped up the stairs and along the first floor landing.

Later Todd was to realise just how lucky he'd been, because despite Tanya's plotting nobody could have planned for things to work out as well as they did. At the exact moment that he was leading Davina into his and Tanya's bedroom Jay came out of one of the bathrooms and saw the pair of them. He stood stock still and for a moment his usual mask of indifference slipped. Todd saw anger flare in his eyes and his full mouth tightened, while his hands clenched at his sides, his whole body rigid. Next to him Todd could feel Davina's reaction as she too grew tense and gazed at Jay.

'Hi!' said Todd as casually as he could manage. 'Great party.'

'Glad you think so,' said Jay, clearly forcing himself to relax. 'Enjoy yourselves you two.' He gave Davina a tight smile and then brushed past the pair of them, hurrying down the staircase and into the mass of people below as though anxious to turn his back on them. At that moment Todd knew that Tanya had been right. Jay did care for Davina, he cared for her more than he wanted to admit, which was astonishing. Just the same, it wasn't going to stop Todd from having a good time with her.

'In we go then,' he said briskly, opening the bedroom door. 'I'll lock the door to make sure we're not interrupted.'

'No, don't lock the door,' exclaimed Davina. 'I don't want to feel trapped.'

'I thought you might be on edge if people could get in,' explained Todd.

'I'll be more relaxed if I know I can get out quickly,' said Davina apologetically.

Todd felt a bit surprised. 'I didn't realise I was that frightening. But, if that's what you want I'll leave it unlocked.' And with that he reached out and began to remove Davina's clothes.

When they were both undressed Davina stood hesitantly by the bed. She wasn't quite sure how all this had happened. She liked Todd, in fact there was more warmth about him than there was about Jay, but she'd never considered him as a sexual partner. Yet somehow here she was, standing naked in a bedroom with him, and there was no point in denying that she was excited.

'Come here,' said Todd, patting the bed before lying flat on his back on the bedspread with his knees drawn up. 'Kneel over my face, honey,' he said urgently. 'You can lean back against my knees to make yourself comfortable.'

Davina did as he suggested but as she knelt over his face her legs were stretched wide apart and she realised that her vulva was directly over his mouth. He reached up with one hand and lightly tugged on her pubic hair. 'Now relax,' he reminded her, and as she obeyed, moving herself until his knees were supporting her back, her vulva was opened wide for him and he pushed his tongue deep inside her vagina while at the same time parting her sex lips with one hand and sucking on her rapidly hardening clitoris.

Davina's body started to quake. Every muscle in her belly seemed to be moving, slithering in excited anticipation as her pleasure grew. She felt her nipples start to ache and her breasts begin to swell. Todd's tongue was flicking in and out of her moist entrance, occasionally swirling around inside, touching the sensitive nerve endings near the entrance, which made her lower body jump as her pleasure deepened.

'Rub your own breasts,' he murmured, lifting his head for a moment. 'Play with your nipples. Stretch them out as far as you can.'

Davina's fingers were shaking as she grasped the rigid tips. Immediately sparks of heat shot through her and the aching deepened. With a soft cry she cupped her breasts with her hands, rubbing her palms over the whole area, her fingers tightening and releasing the burgeoning flesh in a rhythm that she quickly discovered suited her.

Todd sucked harder on her clitoris and she tensed in anticipation of an orgasm, but just as she was about to come he removed his mouth and she uttered a tiny wail of disappointment as the sensations started to die away. 'I was coming then,' she cried.

'Yeah, I know, that's why I stopped. We don't want it over too soon, do we, honey?'

Davina wasn't sure that he was right. Every part of her was ready for an orgasm and she pinched harshly at her nipples, occasionally running her hands over her ribcage and down her belly while Todd once more began to suck on her hard clitoris. Again the incredible sensations mounted and her whole body stiffened. 'Don't stop this time,' she begged as she increased the pressure of her hands on her swollen breasts. 'It feels so good.'

'That's right, don't keep the lady waiting,' drawled Jay from the bedroom doorway and Davina stared at him in horror as he walked over to the bed, standing at the head so that he could watch her. 'Keep going,' he urged her. 'Let me see you come. You've no idea how exciting you look.'

Davina was stunned to realise that his presence was increasing her excitement. She felt as though she would go out of her mind with pleasure. Seeming to sense this, Todd opened her sex lips even wider and flicked the point of his tongue up and down her soaking inner channel before suddenly stabbing it down on the highly sensitive clitoris. Immediately her body spasmed furiously and she threw her head back with a scream of ecstasy as every nerve ending in her body sent flashing messages of glorious sensual pleasure to her brain, and her muscles tightened and released in almost painfully sharp contractions.

When the last delicious flickers of pleasure were fading Davina pulled herself upright, but to her surprise Todd's mouth returned to her highly sensitive flesh and he began to re-arouse her.

'No, I can't come again,' she cried.

'Sure you can,' said Jay, never taking his eyes off her. 'Let's see how quickly you manage it.'

To her shame Jay was proved right because within seconds she felt her juices start to flow again. This time Todd allowed his teeth to graze the side of the stem of her clitoris, which caused her to jerk forward as an almost painfully sharp orgasm ripped through her, an orgasm that went on and on until she heard herself groan with a mixture of delight and despair.

'That's better,' murmured Jay as she straightened up

and their eyes met. 'That's what I like to see, people enjoying themselves at my parties.' Davina couldn't think what to say and before she had a chance to respond he was gone, leaving her and Todd alone in the room.

Todd gently moved Davina around so that she was beneath him and then he put his hands beneath her buttocks, helping her to take her weight on her arms and toes so that he could use his mouth and tongue on the whole of the area between her thighs, re-exciting her wanton flesh for a third time. Finally he eased her down onto the bed and, taking his weight on his elbows, thrust slowly inside her, working his hips steadily and watching her carefully. It wasn't until she came again that he allowed his own pleasure to spill.

When it was over Davina lay motionless, her body covered in perspiration, her limbs weak. She felt utterly sated and was delighted when, unlike Jay in London, Todd wrapped his arms around her, cradling her against him while her body slowly recovered from the excitement. 'You were great,' he whispered against her ear. 'It turned you on, didn't it, having Jay walk in on us?'

'I suppose so,' she conceded.

'Hell, that's nothing to be ashamed about. It shows that you'd fit in with our games.'

'But it's wrong,' protested Davina.

Todd chuckled quietly. 'What do you mean, "wrong"?'

'It's not what sex is meant to be about.'

'Says who?'

'I don't know,' she admitted helplessly. 'I suppose what I mean is, it isn't what I've always believed sex was about.'

'Yeah, well maybe you should think again,' suggested Todd.

Davina wondered if he was right. Certainly if anyone had told her a few weeks earlier that she'd have been behaving like this she'd never have believed them. It was amazing how skilful a lover Todd had been, but even more amazing was the way she'd reacted to having Jay watch. Never in her wildest dreams would she have considered herself an exhibitionist, but despite this she'd enjoyed having him there, knowing that he was being turned on by her excitement.

'I don't understand what's happening to me,' she confessed to Todd as she began to dress.

'Don't think about it,' said Todd firmly. 'Just go with it, sugar. If it feels right for you that's fine. The only rule is never do anything that makes you feel uncomfortable.'

'Never?' she asked with interest.

Todd looked thoughtful. 'I guess sometimes it's good to push the envelope a bit.'

'Push the envelope?'

'Yeah, you know, extend the boundaries, discover more about yourself.'

'I can't believe there's much more to discover.'

Todd smiled at her. 'Hang around with us a while longer and you'll learn differently,' he assured her.

When they rejoined the party and Davina went in search of Phil, Todd's words echoed in her head. They excited her because she had a feeling that she was going to hang around with them for a few more weeks and in the process would discover a lot more about herself. She had no doubt that Jay would expect this, and if he imagined for one moment that she was going to refuse to do anything and vacate the cottage he had another think coming.

'There you are,' said Phil, catching sight of her. 'Where have you been?'

'Here and there,' she said vaguely. 'What about you? The last I saw of you, you were disappearing into the billiard room with Pattie.'

She wanted to laugh at the expression on Phil's face. Clearly he hadn't noticed her in there and didn't quite know how to reply. 'We went out through the French windows and into the garden for some air,' he mumbled.

'It looks as though it did you good. Your colour's excellent,' said Davina dryly.

'So's yours,' retorted Phil.

'Then you were right and I was wrong,' said Davina sweetly. 'The party seems to have been good for both of us.'

'I think we'd better go now,' said Phil firmly, and when Davina glanced over her shoulder for one last look, she caught Jay's eye. He and Tanya were dancing together, Jay's hands roaming over her in a manner that made it clear that they would probably be heading upstairs soon, but the look that he gave Davina made her heart race. He might as well have shouted across the room to her because the message was very clear. Now that he'd seen her and Todd together and had watched, he was going to expect more, much more.

Chapter Nine

By mid-afternoon on the following Monday, Davina had decided that Jay wasn't going to visit her. In a way she was quite relieved. The memory of him standing watching her as she writhed in ecstasy beneath Todd's expert ministrations was highly embarrassing, but she was also disappointed. The truth was she'd become hooked on his visits and the excited anticipation that she always felt as she waited to hear how her rent was to be paid.

Determinedly she picked up her pencil and began her third attempt at a jacket for the book of children's fairy stories. In her mind she could see how it should look but the practicalities of it were eluding her. 'You look busy,' said Jay, and Davina spun round in astonishment, her pencil flying out of her hand.

'How did you get in here?'

'Your back door was unlocked so I walked in. You should be more careful. There are all kinds of perverts out there, you know.'

'I'm very well aware of that.'

'You sure as hell are.'

'Is there something I can do for you?' she asked.

'Naturally. Letting Todd give you endless orgasms doesn't count as rent money I'm afraid.'

'I might have known you'd bring that up at the first opportunity. I'm surprised it made any impression on you. I thought that sort of thing was commonplace in your life.'

'What sort of thing?'

'Having sex with comparative strangers.'

'Is that how it seemed to you? That you were having sex with a comparative stranger? No wonder you were so excited. Take it from me, honey, I don't go in for sex with strangers. Sex with my friends, yeah, for sure, but strangers, that can be dangerous.'

Davina was immediately thrown on the defensive.

'You know perfectly well Todd's not a complete stranger. That wasn't what I meant.'

'Then what did you mean?' He looked at her keenly.

'I meant that there's no feeling between us, that ...'

'That it was just a fuck, huh?'

'That's not how I'd put it.'

'It's what it seemed like, and good luck to you. You were sure having a great time. Here, you might need this later.' Bending down he retrieved her pencil.

Davina snatched it out of his hand. 'As you can see, I am busy. What did you want to tell me?'

'The landlord doesn't even get offered a cup of coffee any more?'

Davina sighed. 'All right, I give in. Would you like a coffee?'

Jay shook his head. 'I've just had one.'

She was livid. 'Then why did you say you wanted one?'

'I didn't, I pointed out that I hadn't been offered one. You should listen more carefully to what I say.'

'You're always playing games, aren't you?' said Davina, thoroughly exasperated. 'Either word games or sex games. Don't you take anything seriously?'

'My work,' he said shortly.

'Now that we've established you don't want coffee, what is it you do want?'

'I've come to invite you over to the house tonight. Tanya and Pattie are having a girls' evening. I want you to join them.'

'You want me to spend an evening with Pattie and Tanya in payment for the cottage?' she asked incredulously. Jay nodded. 'How will that benefit you?'

'I'll be there.'

Suddenly Davina began to understand what he really meant. 'You're not talking about an evening spent discussing clothes, boyfriends and knitting patterns, are you?'

'Nope.'

'Perhaps you'd like to tell me what you are talking about?'

'Nope.'

'Do I have to wear anything special?'

'Wear what you like, as long as it comes off easily.'

Davina frowned. 'You say it's a girls' evening, what exactly do you mean by that, Jay?'

'Can't you guess?'

Davina remembered watching Pattie and Tanya together after that unforgettable dinner a couple of weeks earlier. She remembered that she'd been excited by what she'd seen, but at the same time she wasn't certain that she could let other women see her naked or bring her to a climax, especially if Jay was present.

'What's the matter?' His voice was sharp.

'I'm not very good at girls' evenings.'

'I'm not asking you to be good at it. Truth to tell, I'd prefer you to be bad!'

'Please, don't ask this of me,' said Davina quietly. 'It's not something that I'm comfortable with.'

'That's too bad.' He sounded genuinely regretful. As Davina watched, he walked slowly around the studio. 'I don't think I'd have any trouble letting this place out. You can't be the only artist around here and this is a great studio. How long would it take you to find somewhere else to live?'

'You'd really do that, wouldn't you?' she said bitterly. 'If my uncle had known the truth about you he'd never have left me in this situation. How did you manage to fool him?'

'He knew all about me,' Jay assured her. 'Maybe it was you he didn't know so well.'

Suddenly Davina was determined Jay wasn't going to get his way. 'All right,' she said shortly. 'If that's what you want, I'll come.'

'I don't want you doing anything you're not comfortable with.'

Davina glared at him. 'Yes you do. That's precisely what you enjoy, watching me do things that aren't in my nature.'

'When I watched you with Todd it looked as though it was very much in your nature. He didn't coerce you, did he? After all, what kind of hold has he got over you?'

'That was different!'

'In what way?' he asked curiously.

'It just happened.'

'Is that a fact? Hardly an excuse in a court of law.'

'I'm not in a court of law,' Davina reminded him. 'I'm in my own cottage and ...'

'You're in my cottage, Davina. You're my tenant.'

'A fact that you never let me forget. Look, now that I've said I'll come over tonight do you think you could go? I'd really like to get on with my work.'

'Sure, suits me fine. I'll tell Pattie and Tanya to expect you around eight. You'd better eat first, there'll be plenty of wine but we'll have eaten earlier.'

Davina nodded, certain that she would have very little appetite by the evening. 'Perhaps you'd care to leave the way you came in, like some kind of sneak-thief,' she suggested sweetly.

'Make sure you lock up after me or someone even worse might creep in.'

'I find that difficult to imagine,' replied Davina. All the same, when he'd gone she carefully locked the back door and checked the windows before settling back to work.

Unfortunately Jay's orders had left her mind in turmoil and she found it impossible to concentrate on her work. More and more he was intruding on her thoughts. Ever since he'd made love to her in London she'd found it impossible to get him out of her mind. She wondered why it was that after such an incredible and tender session of lovemaking he hadn't attempted to touch her again, and neither had he referred to it. It was as though it had never happened, yet it had and she was sure it had meant as much to him as to her.

'You're fooling yourself, Davina,' she said aloud. 'If it had really meant anything to him he'd have taken you to bed again by now, and he'd have been annoyed when he saw you with Todd.' Hard as it was to accept this, she knew that she must. For Jay she was simply someone to toy with, someone to confuse and trick with his strange brand of eroticism that expressed itself in sexual and mental games.

When it was time for her to leave for the girls' evening she was in a state of turmoil. In the end she settled for wearing a button-through dress with soft pleating and short sleeves. The tan and cream check suited her and as her legs were brown from the summer sun she didn't bother with stockings. Also, aware of what probably lay ahead, she wore her most attractive silk bra and pantie set, determined that the other two women wouldn't make her look unsophisticated.

She was surprised by the warmth with which Pattie and Tanya welcomed her to the house. Pattie smiled broadly and gestured towards the stairs. 'Would you like to come up? We're all in the master bedroom.'

'All?' asked Davina.

'That's right,' said Tanya calmly. 'I thought Jay had explained to you that the two men will watch us.'

'I knew Jay was going to, but not Todd.'

'Does it make a difference?' asked Tanya.

'I suppose not,' admitted Davina. Her stomach felt tight with apprehension but she knew that she had to go on with this. The walk up two flights of stairs seemed an incredibly long one, and when she entered the master bedroom and saw Jay and Todd seated on a high-backed, two-seater settee on the far side of the room she almost bolted. Tanya, who seemed to sense her unease, hastily closed the door and turned the key in the lock.

'We don't want Clive walking in on us, do we?' she said sweetly.

'No,' said Davina, remembering the way Jay had walked in on her and Todd.

'Here, would you like a sherry?' asked Pattie, holding out a glass, and Davina took it gratefully, her hand shaking a little.

'There's nothing to be nervous about, honey,' remarked Pattie, stepping out of her skin-tight jeans and pulling off her figure-hugging halter top so that she was left standing in a satin bra and G-string. 'We girls always have great fun, ain't that a fact, Tanya?'

Tanya nodded and when she removed her shift dress Davina was surprised to see that she was totally naked beneath it. 'Take off your clothes,' Tanya urged her. 'Then we'll all lie on the bed and relax.'

A few minutes later Davina found herself sitting self-consciously on the bed between the other two women while they kissed over the top of her body. She could tell that they were at ease with each other; the kiss was gentle yet erotic and despite her nerves she felt her body begin to stir. While continuing to kiss Pattie, Tanya started to lightly finger Davina's breasts, her hands playing over the small mounds until the nipples stiff-ened beneath her caress.

Soon the two American girls broke away from each other and while Tanya continued playing with Davina's upper body, Pattie positioned herself lower down the bed and pressed lightly against the inner creases at the top of Davina's thighs.

Immediately her body responded, sparks of excite-ment flared in her and her belly tightened. Her breasts were beginning to ache and she gave a soft moan of pleasure when Tanya started to use her mouth on them, licking delicately around the areolae. Then, as Pattie's fingers began to creep inexorably nearer to Davina's swelling clitoris, Tanya suddenly nipped on the rigid tip of Davina's left nipple causing her to cry out with shock.

At the sound of her cry Pattie's fingers moved more rapidly, rubbing against the damp flesh and circling round and round the pulsating clitoris as Davina's body began to arch up off the bed. She felt her toes curling upwards, a sure sign that her climax was imminent.

She was so lost in the delicious sensations that she didn't realise Tanya was moving until the dark-haired girl knelt over Davina's head, lowering herself so that Davina could caress her with her tongue. 'Touch me exactly as Pattie's touching you,' she urged her. 'Imitate every move she makes.'

Davina groaned. She'd been so lost in the pleasure the two young women were giving her that she didn't want to be distracted, but at the same time she was unexpectedly excited by the realisation that she could give Tanya the same kind of pleasure she was receiving herself.

Pattie, who'd paused for a moment while Tanya explained what she wanted Davina to do, now inserted the tip of her tongue into Davina's damp entrance and Davina immediately did the same to Tanya. Then, as Pattie's tongue swirled lightly over the delicate skin between the inner lips she copied that too. Suddenly Tanya began to whimper and her body trembled delicately.

For several minutes Pattie continued to lick and suck at Davina and Davina reciprocated on Tanya until the pair of them were both on the brink of orgasm. Finally, Pattie closed her mouth over Davina's clitoris and the surrounding flesh and at exactly that moment Tanya lowered herself, so that Davina could do the same to her. As Davina's body spasmed helplessly, racked by waves of delicious pleasure, Tanya too shook and cried in ecstatic relief.

'My turn now,' cried Pattie excitedly, sliding herself up the bed, and Tanya put two cushions beneath Pattie's stomach before walking across the room to fetch some items from a small case on the dressing table. When she returned she handed a soft jelly-like vibrator to Davina. 'I'm going to put these vibrating love-balls inside Pattie,' she whispered. 'They always drive her mad. At the same time I'll finger her and when I give you the nod, part the cheeks of her bottom and slide that inside her. Here, you'll need to lubricate it first.'

Davina stared at the strange contraption. 'Won't it hurt her?' she asked nervously.

Tanya shook her head. 'I told you, she loves it. Be sure to turn it onto the fastest setting.'

'What are you two plotting?' asked Pattie, her voice muffled in the duvet.

'You'll have to wait and see,' Tanya teased her, and as Davina watched, Todd's wife slid her hands skilfully beneath the Californian girl's lower body. After briefly caressing her belly and hips her hands moved, and Davina realised that she was inserting the vibrating balls.

'Oh God, that's delicious,' groaned Pattie as she started to shake.

Despite the fact that she'd already come Davina was aroused again. The sight of the blonde girl's taut buttocks and slender hips trembling with every pulsation was making her want further satisfaction. Without thinking she began to stroke her own breasts, sighing with pleasure as she did so.

'Greedy!' said Tanya as she laughed softly. 'Remember now, watch me for the signal.'

Ashamed of her own wantonness, Davina watched closely. As Pattie's groans increased she began to wriggle frantically, pressing herself down on the bed for further stimulation while Tanya's nimble fingers worked between her thighs. Suddenly Tanya nodded at Davina. Davina hesitated for a second, but when Tanya shot her a glance of puzzled impatience she parted Pattie's buttocks and carefully eased the tip of the strange vibrator inside the tiny puckered opening that seemed far too small for it.

'Oh yes!' screamed Pattie, and encouraged by this Davina turned the switch to the highest setting. Immediately she felt the vibrator shaking in her hand and she realised that the blonde was being stimulated in every possible way, with the vibrating balls deep inside her vagina and this squirming, probing vibrator titillating the walls of her rectum.

Davina could imagine the delicious hot tightness that Pattie must be feeling and as her cheeks flushed she realised that she was going to come too. Just at that moment, Pattie gave an ear-splitting scream of satisfaction as her tormented body finally found relief. Immediately Davina used her fingers to pinch her own nipples hard, one after the other, triggering the climax that she'd sensed was so near.

As Pattie remained slumped face down on the bed Tanya looked at Davina and smiled. 'That really turned you on, didn't it?'

'Yes,' whispered Davina.

'Girls' nights are always fun.'

Davina didn't answer because she couldn't believe what had happened. Never, for one moment, had she expected to be so turned on by the sight of another woman coming but that, coupled with all the divine things that the two Americans had done to her, had provided her with incredible pleasure.

'What now?' she asked.

Jay got to his feet. 'Now you leave,' he said, his voice deeper and thicker than usual.

'Leave?' Davina felt stunned.

'Yeah, the girls' night's over. It's time for mixed doubles and I'm afraid there aren't enough men to go round. You'd better get back to your little cottage, Davina. At least you know it's yours for another few days.'

Pattie and Tanya were both sitting up now, leaning back against piles of pillows and idly stroking each other's bodies as they watched Davina through half-closed eyes, their sexual satisfaction evident. Despite this, Davina knew that they would soon be enjoying yet more pleasure, pleasure given to them by Jay and Todd. It was a pleasure that she wished she could stay and share.

'Your clothes are there,' said Jay helpfully, pointing to where they lay in a heap on the floor.

'I know,' muttered Davina and reluctantly began to dress.

Finally, when every button on her dress had been done up, she started for the door and as she looked back to say goodbye she saw Jay reaching out for Tanya. There was a look on his face that she'd never seen before, dominating, almost frightening and yet incredibly sexual.

'You'd better go,' he said curtly. 'I'm about to take Tanya to my room.'

Confused, her mind still reeling from all that had

happened, Davina fled, but once back at the cottage all she could do was wonder what was going on between Jay and Tanya.

As Jay dragged Tanya into his bedroom she felt a frisson of fear run through her. He was handling her far more roughly than usual and although she was excited she was also surprised. It wasn't the way he normally behaved when they were alone together.

Without a word to her he shut the bedroom door, pulled her arms behind her back and fastened her wrists with the cord of his dressing gown. She made a mild sound of protest but he ignored her, pushing her across the carpet and up against one of the four wooden bedposts that supported the rich brocade canopy. Swiftly he fastened a belt around her waist so that she was completely helpless and she looked at him in astonishment.

'What are you doing, Jay?'

'We've done this before,' he muttered thickly.

'Only when we're all together,' she protested.

Jay's eyes were hard. 'What's the matter? You're not afraid of me, are you?'

The truth was, she did feel a little afraid. She enjoyed mild S&M in a group but right now she had no protection. She suddenly recognised how powerful Jay was and was about to tell him to stop when his hands started to caress her bare breasts and she realised that she was already excited. He stroked the soft flesh lightly, almost tenderly and she felt her fear ease. Her head fell back against the bedpost and her eyelids closed. Just as she started to murmur with pleasure he flicked sharply at each of her erect nipples and she squealed with pain. 'That hurt.'

'It turned you on though,' he muttered, thrusting a hand between her thighs, and almost immediately she felt him push two fingers inside her while his other hand continued to pinch and flick at her throbbing breasts. The result was an extraordinary mixture of pain and pleasure that rapidly aroused her. 'You see, fear can be an aphrodisiac,' said Jay, and she knew that he was right.

When he knelt on the floor and roughly parted her legs she tensed as his mouth moved hungrily over the delicate area between. His tongue stabbed at her tender flesh and she felt his teeth grazing the very tip of her throbbing clitoris. With a cry she was racked by a sharp, intense orgasm. Her body tried to jack-knife forward but the belt cut into her flesh and she hastily straightened up.

For half an hour he kept her there, alternating tender caresses with harsher touches, occasionally slapping at her bare flesh with the backs of his fingers, causing her skin to redden and a strange hot, dark pleasure to course through her veins. She lost count of how many times she came, but she knew that the pleasure was different because it continued to be tinged with fear.

Finally he unfastened the belt and threw her onto the bed, but although she begged for him to untie her hands he refused. Instead he turned her roughly onto her stomach, pulled her hips into the air, parted the cheeks of her bottom and as she stiffened in protest he spread lubricating jelly around the tiny opening. Then he thrust hard inside her, while with his free hand he reached beneath her so that as he invaded the forbidden entrance he distracted her from the initial discomfort by massaging her clitoris in the way that she liked best.

She was whimpering and crying now, but to her shame she didn't want him to stop. The whole experience was mind-blowing and when he finally came she fell forward onto the bed as he allowed her to take almost his full weight. For a few moments they lay in silence. His mouth was resting on the nape of her neck and to her astonishment she heard him murmur, 'Davina.'

Eventually she managed to wriggle away from beneath him. 'Please untie me now, Jay,' she said firmly. 'My shoulders are aching.'

He looked at her in surprise. 'Sure, I forgot.' She felt his hands fumbling at the sash and then, at last, her wrists were free and he carefully massaged them as the blood returned. 'You weren't too uncomfortable, were you?' he asked.

'Some of the time,' she confessed. 'But it made for brilliant sex.'

He nodded grimly. 'Yeah, I guess it did.'

'You know, Jay, that's the first time that I've felt you weren't really thinking of me when we were having sex together,' said Tanya. 'It was as though you were angry, as though you were forcing climaxes from me as a kind of punishment.'

Jay shook his head. 'Why would I be angry with you?'

'I don't think you were. I don't think it had anything to do with me.'

'Look, if you didn't like it I'm sorry,' he said shortly. 'I imagined it would make a change. If I stepped out of line I apologise.'

Tanya stroked the side of his face in a tender caress. 'You didn't step out of line and I'm not complaining, but be honest with me, Jay. You weren't thinking of me, were you?'

'Maybe not.'

'Who were you thinking of?'

He gave a short laugh. 'Myself, of course.'

Tanya shook her head. 'You were thinking about Davina.'

'Why the hell should I be thinking about Davina?'

'Because you were turned on watching her with Pattie and me. You'd have liked to bring her in here and do all the things to her that you did to me. You want her, but you want to punish her for making you want her. Why do you think it's wrong for you to fancy her?'

Jay's voice was low. 'I can't understand myself. When I took her to London we spent the night together. It was good, in fact I'd go so far as to say it was great. The problem is she's the kind of girl who expects commitment and I haven't got time for that. I just want to get her out of my system. Maybe then I can stop thinking about her.'

'Why not live with her for a while?' suggested Tanya. 'I take it you're bored with Pattie?'

'We're bored with each other. She thinks I don't know that she's been screwing Phil at every possible opportunity. Talk about an insult. You'd think she'd find someone with more intelligence.'

'Maybe it's because he's so different from you,' suggested Tanya. 'Perhaps she wants commitment as well.'

'No, she wants to be a good Bostonian wife. Can you imagine it? I'd be a laughing stock with her at my side.'

'Then perhaps it's time you told her that,' said Tanya quietly. 'Not that Todd married me because he thought I'd fit in to Bostonian society, quite the opposite I should imagine.'

'That was different,' said Jay, with one of his rare smiles. 'He fell in love with you.'

'Suppose you fell in love with Davina? Would that be such a dreadful thing?'

Jay looked horrified. 'I haven't fallen in love with her. I'm obsessed with her, but I guess that's because she's a Brit and different. I want to break through that cool exterior, show her that she's no different from the rest of us. Once I've done that there'll be no mystery left and I'll be free.'

'So you want to destroy her in order to concentrate on your work, is that it?'

Jay pulled a face. 'You make me sound pretty damn selfish.'

'I think you are selfish,' said Tanya. 'I suppose you've had to be in order to get on as fast as you have, but maybe it's time to slow down a little.'

'At thirty? I'll think about it in another ten years.'

'Davina won't be around in another ten years,' Tanya pointed out.

'Why do you keep on about her?' he asked irritably. 'Like I said, I just want her out of my system and to get my life back on track again.'

'Perhaps you'll find that even if you succeed in making her more like yourself you still won't be free of her. Maybe possession will increase your obsession, what then?'

'I'll have to make damn sure she leaves the cottage so I won't have to see her again.'

'How do you propose to do that?'

'I'm sure I can come up with some demand that she'll refuse. Luckily the wording of the will gives me the scope to do that.'

Tanya curled herself up into a small ball and lay with her naked back against Jay's bare chest. He flung one large left arm over her and she felt a little of the tension drain out of him. 'You don't think much of me, do you?' he asked quietly.

'That's where you're wrong,' said Tanya seriously. 'I like you a lot, Jay. That's why I don't want you to mess up your life.'

'Then help me,' Jay urged her.

'How?'

'I've been thinking about it and while I was watching you girls tonight I realised that although Davina's always initially reluctant to reveal her sexuality, once she gets going she's pretty abandoned. I want to really tear the veil away, show her the unvarnished truth about herself. It'll be exciting as hell to watch and afterwards she'll probably be so ashamed she'll want to get away from me, which will solve the problem.'

'And how do you intend to do this?' asked Tanya, intrigued.

'I thought the four of us would use her for our entertainment,' he said softly, his breath ruffling Tanya's hair.

She wriggled slightly, her buttocks pressing into his stomach and she felt his penis start to stir. 'You know, that sounds exciting but I can't imagine how you'd get her to take part.'

'That's where you come in,' he explained. 'You'll have to go over to the cottage, say Thursday night, and ask her to do a drawing for you from a photograph that you've brought. Then, when she asks to see the photograph, you'll have to say that you've left it back at the house. Offer to go and get it, that would be the natural thing to do, but knowing Davina she'll offer to come back here with you and save you the trip. Then, when she follows you in through the front door, Todd and I will grab her.'

All the time he was talking Tanya could feel his erection growing, pressing between her buttocks, and she realised that just the thought of it was exciting him. 'You can't force her to take part,' she protested.

'Gee, what kind of a guy do you think I am? I won't have to force her, you wait and see. Sure she'll be frightened at first but once we get her going she won't leave even when I offer her the door.'

'Are you sure of that?' asked Tanya.

'You're goddam right I'm sure.'

'Have you discussed this with Todd?'

Jay sighed. 'Can't you make a decision for yourself, Tanya? You're a big girl now, or at least a grown-up,' he added, as his hands travelled over her slight body.

'I'm happy to do it,' she assured him. 'I only wondered what Todd thought of the idea.'

'I'll ask him later tonight. I don't see why he won't go along with it. As long as he knows Davina can go if she likes he'll probably think it sounds like fun. It'll make a change for all of us, not just Davina.'

'In the meantime, what are you going to do with that?' asked Tanya mischievously, reaching behind her back and running her fingers up and down his shaft.

'What would you like me to do with it?'

'Do you really need to ask?' laughed Tanya, and

turning towards Jay she pushed him onto his back before straddling his body, balancing herself so that his glans was just touching her clitoris. She moved her hips back and forth, feeling the first tremulous stirrings of excitement deep within her.

Jay looked up at her, his hazel eyes gleaming, and reaching up he caressed her small breasts, only this time his touch was light against the previously abused flesh. 'Touch yourself,' he urged as she felt her climax approaching. 'Lick your finger and then run it in circles around your clitoris. I love the expression on your face when you do that.'

Tanya was trembling violently, her orgasm drawing nearer and nearer, and she could hardly bear it because her nerve endings were still so sensitive. Obeying him only increased her pleasure and she obediently licked the middle finger of her right hand and then leant back slightly on his erection, so that he could see her masturbating herself.

The moment she started tracing the circle around her clitoris the contractions started deep within her and she felt her whole body tighten. 'I'm coming,' she warned him.

Jay watched. 'Keep looking at me as you come,' he commanded her.

Normally Tanya closed her eyes at the height of ecstasy and it felt extraordinary to force herself to keep them open, to stare into the depths of Jay's eyes and watch his excitement grow as her movements became more and more frantic until finally she was coming, her whole body shaking. Still their eyes remained locked together until his body jerked beneath her and she felt him come once more, spilling his hot seed deep inside her in an unexpected second climax.

'Fantastic!' he murmured as she slid off him, and for a moment his hand wandered down her spine before he tapped her lightly on the bottom. 'Time to get back to the other two.'

'And you still want to go through with your plan, do you?' she asked, wondering why it was that her body still seemed to want further stimulation.

'You bet I do.'

When they reached the door to the master bedroom where Todd and Pattie were still busy, Tanya turned to Jay. 'You're the most incredible lover I've ever had, Jay. If only you were a warmer person you'd be a helluva catch.'

'That's the whole point, isn't it?' he said lightly. 'I don't want to be caught.'

Late that night Tanya told Todd everything that had occurred between her and Jay. To her surprise he didn't make any protest about Jay's plan for Thursday night. In fact, he seemed quite turned on by it. He was even more turned on by what she told him Jay had done to her and as soon as she'd finished talking he took her swiftly and urgently, and this time after she'd climaxed and was lying in his arms she felt totally relaxed and ready for sleep. She realised then that like most women she needed more than Jay was able to offer. No matter how great the sexual pleasure he gave, he left an emotional void, a void that men like Todd were able to fill.

'We'll have to help Davina,' she murmured sleepily.

'To catch Jay you mean?' asked Todd.

'No, of course not. To get through Thursday night.'

'Sure,' agreed Todd. 'I'm looking forward to it. The way I see it Jay's right. We're all going to have one helluva time.'

Chapter Ten

Davina was surprised to open the door of her cottage and find Tanya standing on the doorstep several days later. Surprised, and also embarrassed because immediately memories of the things that Tanya had done to her came flooding back. Clearly though Todd's wife didn't share her embarrassment. She looked very relaxed and smiled warmly at Davina. 'I hope you don't mind me calling. I've come to ask you a favour.'

'Of course, come in.'

'Hey, this cottage is fabulous. Jay wasn't exaggerating when he described it. May I see your studio?'

Davina nodded, hoping that Tanya didn't know the things that had gone on there between her and Jay. 'I had it built on,' she explained to the American girl. 'Once it was clear that I was settling here, Uncle David suggested I used some of the money from my divorce to build myself a decent studio.'

'No wonder you don't want to move.'

'It's my home.'

'Your art work's incredibly good,' murmured Tanya, looking at various framed drawings and jacket covers from books that Davina had worked on. 'Actually, that's really why I'm here. I want you to do a drawing for me.'

'What kind of drawing?'

'I've got this godson back in the States. He's eight months old now, and incredibly cute. His mother's my best friend. Although she's got loads of photos I thought it would be neat if I sent her a drawing of Sam taken from a photograph. I know she'll love it.'

Davina hesitated. 'I don't usually do portraits.'

'Hey, I don't expect it to be spot on, just an overall impression. Eight months is such a lovely age. He's all chubby and a completely blank canvas. When he's a teenager it might help keep his mother sane!' She laughed.

'I'll do my best. Do you have the photo with you?'

'Sure.' Tanya reached inside the pocket of her jacket and a look of dismay crossed her face. 'Heck, I was sure I'd brought my wallet with me, and the picture's in it. Tell you what, I'll go back and fetch it. It won't take me five minutes. By the way, I'll pay you handsomely for this, I'm not expecting it as a favour.'

Davina felt uncomfortable. 'Honestly, you don't have to pay me. Surely we know each other too well for that.'

'We know each other pretty well,' conceded Tanya. 'All the same, I don't believe that you should use your friends. It'd be like asking Jay to act as our lawyer without us paying him a fee.'

Davina smiled. 'Somehow I can't imagine that happening.'

'No, because we wouldn't dare ask him,' laughed Tanya. 'Look, wait there and I'll run and get the photo.'

Davina shook her head. 'It's all right, I'll come back to the house with you and collect it. Otherwise you'll be doing the walk three times.'

'It's not that far,' protested Tanya.

'It's far enough, and it looks like rain.'

Tanya looked at Davina, who was struck by the

seriousness of her expression. 'Are you really sure you want to come back to the house with me, Davina?'

'Of course, I wouldn't have offered otherwise.' She was surprised that Tanya wasn't more grateful. If anything Todd's wife looked uncomfortable, uneasy, as though what Davina had suggested wasn't what she'd have chosen. Since Davina couldn't think of any possible reason for this she decided that she must be imagining it. Together the two women made their way to the house. To Davina's surprise the front door was open. 'That's a bit careless, isn't it?' she asked.

'I knew I wouldn't be gone long,' explained Tanya, pushing on the door then standing back to let Davina through in front of her.

Rather puzzled by Tanya's attitude, Davina walked into the hall. As the front door slammed shut she was suddenly grabbed from behind by Jay and Todd who each caught hold of one of her arms and then, half-lifting her off her feet, bundled her unceremoniously down the hallway and through into the main drawing room. With a cry of alarm Davina began to kick out.

'Hey, calm down,' said Jay firmly. 'We're not kidnapping you.'

'Let go of me,' shouted Davina. 'I've come here to get a photo from Tanya. What are you two playing at?' Neither man replied, but when Davina saw that Tanya had followed them into the room and was closing the door behind them she stared at her in disbelief. 'You set this up, didn't you?'

'I'm sorry,' murmured Tanya. 'It'll be all right, I promise you. You'll enjoy yourself.'

'I want to go home, now,' shouted Davina.

'If you're still saying that in ten minutes then I'll open the door for you myself,' murmured Jay, as Pattie rose from a chair at the far end of the room.

'You managed it then?' she said to Tanya. 'I wasn't sure she'd come.'

'What *is* this?' Davina's bewilderment was increasing with every second that passed.

'We decided it was time you joined us in one of our games,' said Jay.

'Don't I have any say in the matter?' asked Davina, still struggling.

'Come on, relax,' Todd urged her. 'We're all going to have a terrific time.'

'I prefer to choose how I enjoy myself,' retorted

Davina, and as she felt Jay's hand start to unfasten her dress she kicked out at him.

'Blindfold her,' he said curtly.

'No, don't!' protested Davina.

'Listen, honey,' Todd whispered in her ear. 'There's nothing to be afraid of. You're going to have a really great time, but if you blow it now you might lose everything, and by everything I don't only mean the cottage.'

Davina knew exactly what he meant; he meant Jay, that she'd lose Jay as well. Abruptly she realised that Todd was right, she didn't want that to happen. Jay had completely changed her life and the prospect of never seeing him again didn't bear thinking about.

'All right,' she whispered. 'But if I don't enjoy the game . . .'

'You can go,' said Jay, and the room went dark as a black satin band was pulled over her eyes.

Instinctively she stiffened. 'Easy, honey,' murmured Jay, his mouth against her ear, and as he spoke she felt hands undressing her. Her clothes were swiftly removed and Jay pushed her gently to the ground. She realised that someone had laid cushions on the floor because her body relaxed against the soft plumpness of them. For a few minutes she was left alone, but she could hear the sound of clothes falling to the ground as the others undressed.

'The girls are going to use you to show us what they want us to do to them,' explained Todd. Davina didn't understand at first. Then she felt someone blowing on her nipples, and as they stiffened delicate fingers pulled at the tips and she arched her upper body.

'Do that to me,' she heard Tanya say, and heard too Jay's murmured assent. She was forced to lie, silent and alone, as Jay presumably carried out Tanya's instructions because she heard Todd's wife's tiny sighs of pleasure. She hated being abandoned like this, especially since she couldn't even see, and without thinking she started to pull on her own nipples, but just as the pleasure began Todd's hands restrained her.

'You'll get your turn,' he promised her. 'For now you mustn't touch yourself at all.'

'I'll show you what *I* want,' Davina heard Pattie say. This time Davina's legs were parted and Pattie pulled apart the prone girl's sex lips, sliding a finger inside her and then trailing the moisture upwards in the lightest of caresses, slowly circling the clitoris until Davina felt it growing hard and an ache began between her thighs.

'That's what I want,' murmured Pattie huskily. 'Will you do that to me, Todd?'

'Sure,' agreed Todd, and once more Davina was forced to lie, alone and untouched, while Todd brought Pattie to orgasm. She could imagine the delicious pleasure of that sliding finger bringing sweet release to Pattie's urgent need.

The two women continued to return to Davina, constantly touching her sufficiently to arouse her, but never enough to satisfy, as they demonstrated what particular caress they wanted from the men. Davina lost track of time but she thought that she must have been lying there for at least half an hour when Jay finally called a halt. 'Okay girls, you've had your pleasure. Time to let Davina join in, I think.'

Once more hands touched her body, this time pulling her to her feet. As the blindfold was removed she blinked at the sudden brightness of the room. 'You look hot,' murmured Jay. 'Tell us how you feel.'

Davina didn't know what to say. She stared mutely at him, hoping that he wouldn't force her but his gaze hardened. 'If you want us to give you pleasure then you have to tell us how you feel.'

'My breasts are aching and my belly feels tight,' whispered Davina. 'It's like having an itch and not being able to scratch.'

Todd laughed. 'That sounds like a pretty good description to me.'

'We'll have to help you,' said Jay. 'What do you say, girls?'

'Oh yes,' agreed the two women in unison. 'We'll help you, Davina.' They were standing around her in a circle now, their eyes bright with excitement, a darkly erotic excitement that only increased Davina's desire.

'First I think we should all have a good look at you,' said Jay. 'Bend forward and touch your toes.'

Davina knew that by doing this she would be incredibly vulnerable, exposing herself totally to the keen gaze of the group, but at the same time once she began to bend she felt a peculiar sense of pride in her body and heard Todd give an appreciative murmur.

'Now straighten up and masturbate yourself to orgasm,' Jay ordered her.

Davina parted her legs and slowly allowed her right

hand to stray through her pubic hair and down between her thighs, where the ache was now growing so intense that it was rapidly becoming pain. She was shocked at how swollen her clitoris was and how damp the surrounding flesh. The moment she began to press against her pubic mound she felt her orgasm start to build, and as she allowed her finger to touch the side of her clitoris she came with a speed that totally humiliated her.

'I guess you didn't exaggerate,' remarked Pattie. 'Do you always reach a climax that quickly when you masturbate?'

Davina hung her head. 'No! It was because you'd all been touching me.'

'There's nothing to be ashamed of,' said Todd. 'I love seeing a woman satisfy herself.'

'In that case why don't we get Davina to do it again,' suggested Jay.

Davina shook her head. 'I won't be able to, not that quickly.'

'That's a pity because you have to before the game can move forward.' His face was expressionless but his eyes were sparkling, and Davina could see from his massive erection that he was incredibly aroused by what was happening. Reluctantly at first she allowed her fingers to play over her body, but this time she didn't go near her clitoris, instead she pressed on the soft pubic mound, digging the heel of her hand down into the base of her belly and rocking her hand backwards and forwards. Soon the delicious tingling sensation began and her breathing quickened.

'Look, her nipples are hard again,' exclaimed Pattie.

'Is it okay if I touch them?' Todd asked Jay, who nodded his approval.

Davina continued moving her hand while Todd walked up to her, bent his head and taking the tip of her left nipple between his teeth nipped lightly at the rigid stem. For a few seconds the sensation was uncomfortably sharp, but then his teeth released her and he swirled his tongue around the area where his teeth had been. The combination of sensations, the excitement of being watched and the realisation of what she was doing all combined to bring Davina to a second orgasm, and she gasped aloud as the contractions flooded through her, leaving her weak and trembling.

'Didn't your mother ever tell you that it was wrong

to play with yourself?' enquired Jay as she stood shaking in front of him.

Davina didn't understand. 'What do you mean?'

'I mean you've just done a very bad thing. You'll have to be punished for it.'

'Oh yes!' enthused Pattie. 'I love games with punishments.'

'What kind of a punishment?' asked Davina, beginning to panic.

'Don't worry, there'll be pleasure at the end of it,' Jay assured her, pulling a ladder-backed chair away from the wall and sitting on it. 'Come over here. It seems I'm going to have to teach you how a young English lady should behave.'

Slowly, hesitantly, Davina walked towards him. His eyes were hypnotic and she realised that she wanted him more now than at any other time. When he grabbed at her wrists and pulled her over his lap she uttered a tiny squeal of protest. As he began to spank her rhythmically with his left hand, he eased his right hand beneath her so that he could stimulate her clitoris at the same time. The hand striking the cheeks of her bottom was firm. Each time it fell on her flesh a hot burning sensation coursed through her buttocks, but just as it began to feel like pain his clever fingers would lightly tease and stroke at her clitoris.

Soon she was writhing helplessly on his lap, crying out incoherently as he brought her inexorably closer and closer to orgasm. She was vaguely aware that the other three were watching her but she didn't care; all she was aware of were the incredible sensations that Jay was giving her.

'You're going to come again, aren't you?' he said softly. 'Admit it.'

'Yes, yes,' she groaned.

'This is meant to be a punishment,' he reminded her. 'I forbid you to come.'

It was too late. Almost as soon as the words were out of his mouth her body tightened and thrashed around on his lap. But for the fact that his hands held her tightly, she would have fallen to the floor.

'She disobeyed again!' cried Pattie. 'Did you see that Todd? Tanya? Jay told her not to come and she did.'

'She sure as hell did,' agreed Todd, and Davina felt his hand caress her back for a moment as she remained in an exhausted heap over Jay's bare thighs.

'I'm sorry,' she whimpered, hideously embarrassed at the way she'd lost control of herself. 'I couldn't help it though, it just felt so good.'

'If it felt that good I assume you won't object to further punishment,' said Jay calmly.

Davina rolled over so that she could stare up at him. His face was implacable, his mouth hard and his eyes expressionless. She wondered why it was that she was so attracted to him, why she so desperately yearned for some proof that he felt the same about her. 'I'm not sure I want to be punished any more,' she said slowly.

He raised one eyebrow. 'You mean you're not willing to pay the rent?'

'I thought this was a game that you wanted me to play,' retorted Davina. 'You never said that you were collecting the rent.'

'I'm saying it now.'

Davina was furious. 'That's cheating.'

'How can I cheat at my own game?'

Davina bit on her lower lip. In a way he'd given her an excuse to carry on indulging in the extraordinary sexual excesses that were on offer. Although nervous she had enough confidence in him to believe that she'd never be hurt, but at the same time she was startled by her own responses to all that was going on. Leaving would have saved her further embarrassment, and further self-discovery.

Right now she wasn't too sure that she liked what she was learning about herself. However, by making it a price that she had to pay for her cottage, Jay had offered her a way out. She was utterly determined that he was never going to force her out, which meant that she could take up the challenge and justify it to herself. Only she would ever know that secretly she was excited by the prospect of what was to come.

'Well?' It was clear that he was running out of patience.

'I'll do whatever you say.'

'That's the spirit,' enthused Todd. 'This is going to be great. How about we let the girls choose the punishment this time, Jay?'

'Sounds good to me,' agreed Jay.

Davina scrambled up off his lap and stood facing the rest of the group. Then she waited tensely as Tanya and Pattie surveyed her. 'Let's take her upstairs,' said Pattie.

'We'll use the master bedroom. There's everything we need there.'

Within a few minutes they were all upstairs and again Davina waited to see what the other women wanted to do to her. 'Put the bolster down the middle of the bed,' said Pattie, 'and let's have the cuffs on her wrists.'

Jay quickly drew a pair of chain-linked leather cuffs with adjustable straps from the dressing table drawer and snapped them tightly around Davina's wrists. Her hands were in front of her at waist level. She tugged fiercely but the chain was short and there was very little room for movement. She could see that Jay's erection was still huge. Walking up to her he put his hands on her hips and pulled her against him, allowing the tip of his penis to push against her sex lips until they parted. For a few fleeting seconds he rubbed himself against her until the delicious hot tingles began once more. Then, as her hips gave an involuntary jerk in response, he stopped and stepped away from her again. 'You certainly seem to be enjoying yourself, despite your protestations,' he remarked dryly.

Davina couldn't deny it, but neither could she understand how the mixture of fear and arousal were working such incredible magic on her. She felt like a different person. It was as though every centimetre of her body was more alive than it had ever been before.

It was obvious that Pattie was impatient. 'Come on, she's not meant to be enjoying herself. Get on the bed, Davina, and lie sideways across the bolster so that your buttocks are raised in the air. Keep your face buried in the bedspread, we don't want you peeking.'

Davina started to tremble; it would be like being blindfolded again and she'd found that frightening. Nevertheless she did as she was told. For a few seconds she lay with her face buried waiting for someone to touch her, for the punishment to begin. When Todd's hands suddenly parted the cheeks of her bottom she gave a tiny cry of fright. 'What are you going to do to me?'

'It'll be great,' he promised her. 'Try and relax, that way the pleasure will come sooner.'

'Let me put some of the jelly on her,' said Tanya, and Davina felt her small fingers spreading a lubricating jelly all around the tiny puckered opening between the cheeks of her bottom, occasionally sliding a finger inside and swirling some of the jelly there.

Davina was reminded of when Jay had made love to

her in London and how his finger had invaded her there. At the memory her body began to shake violently. 'It's all right,' Tanya promised her. 'In a few minutes you'll start enjoying yourself.'

'It might be uncomfortable at first,' said Pattie, and her words made Davina tense her muscles.

'That was a stupid thing to say,' commented Todd. 'Now you've made it more difficult for us.'

'And for her,' said Jay. 'I assume that was the idea, Pattie?'

Pattie gave a soft laugh. 'I just don't feel she's being punished sufficiently.'

'I think she is,' said Jay, 'but you're enjoying the punishment, aren't you, Davina? I think you believe you deserve it. You're ashamed of taking pleasure from all this.'

Davina didn't answer him. She simply buried her face deeper in the bedspread and tried to ignore his words, which were horribly near the truth.

'Here we go then,' said Tanya and Davina felt the tip of something large and hard being inserted into her rectum. 'Don't!' she cried, but her words were ignored.

'Breathe through your mouth,' said Jay quietly. 'It will relax all your muscles.'

Davina did as he said, and quickly felt an egg-shaped object slide inside her anus. She gave a gasp but almost before she had time to register what was happening three more oval-shaped balls were inserted inside her and then, as she was trying to adjust to the full feeling, they started to vibrate and she screamed with shock and fear.

'For God's sake relax and enjoy yourself,' said Jay calmly. 'You're your own worst enemy, Davina.'

She didn't know how she could be expected to enjoy it. She felt full and heavy, and the nerve endings inside the delicate walls were being stimulated so much that the resulting sensations were perilously close to pain.

Then, just as she decided that despite her vow she was going to ask to leave, her body adjusted and now the vibrations were causing nothing but pleasure. It was pleasure of the kind she'd never known before, a deep aching pleasure that was tinged with darkness. It felt as though there was something behind her clitoris, something causing tiny electric currents to stimulate it from deep within her pelvis. She squirmed restlessly against the bolster, spreading her legs wide as she tried to open herself up in order that her clitoris could receive the pressure it needed.

'Lie still,' Pattie ordered her.

Davina shook her head. 'I can't. What you're doing to me isn't fair. I have to move.'

'Disobedience again,' remarked Jay. 'Tanya, use this on her. Perhaps it will keep her still.'

Davina had no idea what he meant, she was only aware of her body's burgeoning need for a climax. As a result, when the soft, sensuous latex pleasure-whip was drawn slowly along the length of her spine before being brought down sharply against the cleft at the join of her buttocks, she cried out in stunned incredulity.

After the initial shock of the blow Davina felt the latex whip being moved up and down her spine, so lightly and slowly that it felt like a cruel caress. Then, abruptly, it rose and fell, the end curling round beneath her armpit and catching the side of her breast. She was about to protest, to say that this was no longer a game when she realised that her whole body was tight with excitement.

'It's all right,' whispered Tanya, putting her mouth

close to Davina's ear. 'You're doing really well and Jay's impressed.'

The words were exactly what Davina needed to hear. Now she gave herself over to the extraordinary sensations as the vibrating balls continued their wicked arousal while the alternate trailing motion, followed by a sharp flick of the whip, drove her into a frenzy. She felt as though she was going to burst she was so tight, so excited, and yet the climax that was so near refused to come. She began to sob with frustration, not daring to grind her hips again but beside herself with need.

'I wonder how long we can keep her balanced on the edge?' she heard Pattie ask.

'A long time,' said Tanya. 'We just have to be careful not to overdo anything.'

Davina was unable to suppress a groan of despair and was ashamed to hear the others laugh. Now Jay's hand was buried in the hair at the nape of her neck, his fingers moving over her scalp. 'You want to come, don't you?' he asked. 'Tell me how much.'

'I can't bear it,' groaned Davina. 'It's wicked of you to use me like this. I feel as though I'm going to explode but . . .'

'That's what happens when you disobey,' he reminded her. 'You came when you shouldn't and now you can't come when you need to.'

The teasing continued relentlessly until Davina was crying out. She begged them to touch her between her thighs where she ached so desperately, and where her clitoris was swollen and aching, but they simply increased her torment. Someone, she thought it was Todd, ran a feather along the sole of her foot and up the back of her leg. He twirled it briefly between her thighs but just as she thought it was about to move beneath her he removed it, and it became simply another form of stimulation, driving her to fever pitch.

She began to wonder if they were ever going to stop, if she was ever going to be allowed to climax, but then Jay spoke. 'Turn her onto her back so that the whole of her body's spread along the bolster,' he commanded the others. Breathing heavily, her hands still cuffed in front of her, Davina was rolled over until she was in the required position. Once there she lay staring up at Jay who looked down at her with interest.

'How different you look from when I first saw you,' he said quietly. 'I can remember you so clearly. You were incredibly cool and detached, and when you looked at me I could see you judging me.'

'I wasn't,' she protested.

'It looked as though you were, but then that's the way you English always behave. Well, you should see yourself now. You don't look very cool or controlled at this moment.'

'If I've changed it's your fault,' cried Davina, almost weeping with frustration as he began to lightly stroke her belly with the palm of his hand.

'You must take responsibility for your own actions. Looking at you now most people would say that you're in the throes of incredible pleasure. How can that be anyone's fault? Maybe you've learnt things about your-self you'd rather not have known, but I didn't make you what you are. I simply held the mirror up and showed you the truth.'

Davina began to squirm as his fingers trailed over her hip bones and then down lower, towards the spot where she so desperately wanted to be touched.

'Are you going to let her come now?' asked Todd with interest.

'Yeah, I think it's time,' confirmed Jay.

Davina parted her thighs and he carefully separated her swollen sex lips before holding out his hand to Pattie. 'Give me the ring.'

Davina struggled to sit upright; she wanted to see what was happening, but Todd and Tanya held her down. 'You're doing great,' said Todd encouragingly. 'Don't spoil it.'

'Spread her legs wider apart,' Jay said to Pattie, and now Davina was totally open to him. She felt his fingers move lightly along her inner channel, hesitating slightly at her clitoris, and then she felt a hard ring being pressed over the swollen bud, imprisoning it so that it was totally unprotected.

She began to shake, her belly quaking as she imagined what she must look like to him. As she waited for him to touch her, Tanya began to squeeze Davina's breasts before encouraging her husband to suck on the protruding nipples. The pleasure they were bringing her spread through her entire body, increasing the heavy pressure deep in her belly and she heard Jay laugh softly to himself. 'Give me the feather, Pattie,' he said.

Davina's thighs tensed as she waited for the final gentle caress that would release the orgasm that had been building relentlessly for the past half hour. Jay didn't bother with any preliminaries; instead he moved the point of the feather directly onto the tip of the trapped clitoris and stroked it back and forth. At last the nerve endings exploded in a huge orgasmic spasm that caused Davina to arch her lower body off the bed while Todd and Tanya gripped her tightly by the shoulders. She was crying with gratitude and delirious pleasure, but even as she began to descend from the incredible height of pleasure Jay re-applied the feather. This time he ran the tip around the metal ring that was trapping the swollen bud, circling round and round until the spirals of excitement grew again.

It felt to Davina as though her body was being asked to take more pleasure than was humanly possible but she was so aroused, her nerve endings so sensitive, that within a couple of minutes she was once more racked by an incredibly intense orgasm and heard herself crying out in the throes of her passion. 'Yes! Oh, yes! Yes!' she screamed as she twisted and turned, a helpless prisoner of her own wanton passion.

Finally, as the last tremors died away, the Americans unfastened her wrists and rolled her off the bolster, leaving her lying on the bed. She was vaguely aware that they were talking about her, discussing what had happened.

'I think I'd like to take her now,' said Todd.

Davina felt too exhausted to argue. In any case, she wanted to be filled, wanted to feel a man deep inside her giving her a different kind of orgasm, making her feel fulfilled and in some way helping wipe out the memory of the way she'd just behaved.

'Sorry, she's mine,' said Jay, removing the ring around her clitoris.

'What do you mean she's yours?' asked Pattie sharply. Davina thought that she could detect fear in the young woman's voice.

'Exactly what I say. This is how the game ends. You three can go. Use the blue bedroom, or mine if you like. Davina and I are staying here.'

'That wasn't part of the plan,' protested Pattie.

'It was always part of mine,' said Jay calmly. 'If she'd failed, if she'd asked to leave before this point, then that would have been the end of it but she got this far and that's where I come in.'

Davina knew that she'd only got this far because of

Todd and Tanya's encouragement. There'd been times when her courage had nearly deserted her, when despite the pleasure she'd felt that she should stop. Because of them she'd kept going and now, at last, she was to be rewarded. This was what she'd wanted ever since their trip to London, to have Jay making love to her on his own. She was sure that this time, as then, she would glimpse his true feelings towards her, a truth which she was beginning to believe he was trying to conceal from himself as much as from her. She heard the bedroom door close behind the other three.

'Just the two of us again, Davina,' Jay remarked, grasping her wrists and pulling her to the side of the bed. 'I hope you'll enjoy this as much as you've enjoyed the rest of the game.' Davina was certain that she could see affection in his eyes.

'I know I will,' she whispered.

'Yes,' he muttered, 'but what happens afterwards?'

Chapter Eleven

Sitting on the side of the bed Davina stared up at Jay. Her eyes roamed freely over his body, taking in his flat stomach, narrow hips and tight well-muscled thighs. She was overcome with a desire to give him pleasure, to feel more in control, and sinking slowly to the floor she pushed him round until he was the one sitting on the edge of the bed.

'What the hell is it about you?' he whispered to himself, but Davina didn't even pause to consider what he might mean. She laid her left cheek against his stomach and ran her tongue up the side of his erection, gripping the shaft with her right hand at the same time. His hands caressed her hair and moved down slowly over her shoulders, massaging her gently and carefully.

Moving her head a little she was able to draw him into her mouth, and for the first time tasted the slightly salty clear fluid. She had never done anything like this for Phil, nor had she ever wanted to, but now she wished that she could draw Jay even deeper inside her. Almost without thinking her fingers began to stroke his testicles and she felt them moving and growing. He gave a soft sigh of pleasure then, as she began to run her tongue around the underside of his glans, he pushed her abruptly away.

'I'll come too soon,' he warned her, drawing her upwards onto the bed with him so that they were lying side by side, and she could feel his erection pressing against her lower belly.

Without even waiting to be asked Davina crouched on all fours, easing him slowly inside her and feeling a delicious sensation of fullness as she lowered herself onto his hips. Jay lay quietly for a few moments while Davina rhythmically contracted her internal muscles around him, causing the hot tightness to begin to fill her belly once more. Then he sat up, wrapped his arms around her and, keeping her in position, swung his feet over the side of the bed.

'Wrap your arms round my neck,' he murmured huskily.

Once she was secure he stood up and she clutched him even tighter, wrapping her legs around his back and crossing her ankles. His hands were beneath her buttocks, holding her in place, but she was still grateful when he finally pushed her against the wall of the bedroom. This time he was the one in control, pushing fiercely into her, his fingers digging into her flesh. 'Tighten yourself about me again,' he begged her. 'Milk me until I come.'

Davina was shaking violently with excitement, overwhelmed by it all, and she obeyed gladly. Jay's breathing grew shallow and his normally pale complexion flushed as he drew nearer and nearer to orgasm. Davina knew that she too was about to come. She wriggled against him, pushing her hips away from the wall a little in order to stimulate her clitoris against his pubic bone until, at almost exactly the same moment, they both climaxed. Jay shuddered and groaned while Davina uttered tiny ecstatic cries of delight.

She fully expected Jay to put her down the moment it was over but instead he kept his arms about her and, carrying her back to the bed, laid her down gently on the coverlet before sitting next to her. She saw that he was looking at her with an expression of bewilderment on his face. 'What's wrong?' she asked.

'I don't understand what it is about you,' he murmured. 'Why should you be different?' Davina sensed that it would be better to say nothing, that he was probably talking to himself. She smiled at him, then closed her eyes as his hands caressed her. Finally, he bent down and kissed her softly on the mouth. 'You're incredible,' he said. 'But it would never work.'

Davina frowned. 'What do you mean?'

Abruptly Jay moved away from her and began to dress. 'That was great. I think I could do with a bite to eat now, how about you?' he asked brightly.

She blinked in surprise. The change of mood was so extraordinary it was difficult to take in. 'I'm not hungry.'

'You sure? There's nothing I can get you?'

'Nothing at all.'

'Guess you'll want to be going then.'

'Going?' she asked stupidly.

'Yeah, back to your cottage. The game's over now.'

'The game?' For a moment she'd forgotten how the evening had begun, but then the memories came flooding back. 'I'd forgotten the game,' she confessed.

'Is that a fact? You shouldn't do that, it allows your opponent to win.'

Davina stared at him. 'Are you my opponent?'

Jay nodded. 'Of course. I've been your opponent from the moment your uncle died.'

'And that includes tonight?'

'Sure.'

'I see.'

'What the hell else did you think we were? A couple of starry-eyed lovers?'

Davina wanted to cry, but she wasn't going to give him the satisfaction of knowing how much he'd hurt her because she was certain that this was what he was trying to do. He needed to push her away because he was frightened by the intimacy they'd just shared. 'No,' she said smoothly. 'I never thought that.'

'Good. Guess that's your rent paid for the week then.'

'For the whole week?'

Jay nodded. 'I'll be in touch,' he said abruptly and left the room.

Davina didn't allow herself to cry until she was back in the safety of her own cottage, lying in her own bed, but then she cried for a long time because she didn't know what more she could do if she and Jay were ever going to have a proper relationship.

Jay was already eating breakfast the next morning when Pattie walked into the dining room. 'So, what was it like with her last night?' she asked.

Jay didn't want to answer. The last thing he needed right now was to have to discuss Davina with Pattie. He'd got quite enough on his mind. 'Okay.' His voice was non-committal.

'You seemed pretty exhausted by it all. You didn't even ask if I'd had a good time when I got into bed last night.'

'Are you complaining?'

Pattie pouted. 'I guess I feel kind of ignored,' she admitted.

Jay decided to tell her the truth, but not the whole truth. 'It was good sex.'

'Is that all?'

'Would you clarify what you mean by all?'

Pattie poured herself some coffee, her hand shaking slightly with anger. 'I hate it when you talk to me as though I'm in the witness box. Why should I clarify "all"? You know perfectly well what I mean.'

'I don't.'

'I mean was it special? Did she drive you wild with desire? Or, more excitingly, did you terrify her?'

'Why should I want to terrify her?'

'You tell me,' retorted Pattie. 'You seemed intent on frightening her earlier in the evening. I assumed you carried on in the same way once we'd gone.'

'Then you assumed wrong. We just had sex.'

'But you never "just have sex",' said Pattie. 'You're a sensualist, so tell me what it was like.'

'I haven't asked you to describe what went on between you, Tanya and Todd, have I?'

'No.'

'Then let's leave it, shall we? I've got far more important things on my mind right now than what happened in the bedroom last night.'

Pattie glared at him and he braced himself for further

interrogation but, clearly thinking better of it, Pattie decided to sulk silently instead. That didn't bother Jay, he was totally unaffected by her moods. What bothered him right now was the way he'd felt the previous evening. He'd had it so meticulously planned and had been certain that he would either despise Davina for going along with his game or, if she'd lost her nerve and left, that his interest in her would have vanished. He'd been totally wrong. She'd stayed, but by staying she'd managed to intrigue him even more.

Far worse in his opinion was the fact that when he was finally alone with her, he'd felt a wave of tenderness sweep over him. This was something totally alien to Jay and even now he couldn't quite believe it had happened. He was beginning to think that the wretched girl had cast a spell over him. If that was true then at least the telephone call he'd received from America that morning had shown him a way to break the spell. He despised himself for his own weakness; running away was not his usual method of handling things, but in this case it appeared be the only answer.

'Hi,' said Tanya, wandering into the room. 'Looks

like it's gonna be another great day. Why don't we take a drive into Oxford and see the sights, Jay?'

'Sounds like a good idea, but I'm afraid you'll have to get Todd to take you,' explained Jay, rising to his feet. 'I've been summoned back to the States.'

'Oh no,' groaned Pattie. 'How long will you be gone?'

'A week to ten days, maybe longer.'

'Do you want me to come with you?'

Jay shook his head. 'There's no point. I'll be back here before you notice I'm gone, and I'll be working day and night in any case so you'd be bored out of your skull.'

'Does Davina know?' asked Tanya.

'What's it got to do with her?' The moment he'd spoken Jay realised that his voice was too abrupt and he saw Tanya's eyes widen for a split second. 'I only heard myself this morning,' he continued hastily. 'I guess she'll be pleased to have a break from paying the rent.'

'Are you sure it's that way round?' asked Tanya quietly.

'Meaning?'

'She means are you sure you're not glad to have a break from collecting the rent,' said Pattie sweetly. 'I don't think that can be true, Tanya. He's very secretive about what went on between the pair of them last night. I guess he'll miss her a hell of a lot.'

'Davina seems to obsess you,' said Jay.

'I don't think *I'm* the one who's obsessed with her,' snapped Pattie. 'I saw the way you watched her last night. You wanted us all to play with her but then you got jealous, didn't you? You wanted her to yourself, that's why you sent us all out of the room.'

Jay felt utterly exhausted. He'd never had to handle emotions before, at least not his own, and he was finding it very tiring. 'We've already been over all this. Just drop it, honey.'

'When you get back,' said Pattie slowly, 'I think maybe you're going to have to make a few decisions, Jay.'

'Yeah? About what?'

'I'd rather not say in front of Tanya.'

'Your timing's way off beam, Pattie,' Jay cautioned her. 'When I get back we can discuss anything you like. Right now, I've gotta focus my mind on my work.'

'So you'll be shut in your study all morning?' Pattie's displeasure was obvious.

'Yes,' agreed Jay, but once he'd left the dining room he walked out through the front door and made his way along the gravel path to Davina's cottage. When she opened the door to him he noticed that her eyes were red-rimmed and slightly puffy. Remembering the way he'd behaved after they'd made love he felt a twinge of guilt, which he quickly suppressed. Guilt was a waste of time.

The expression on Davina's face was unfathomable. 'I thought I'd already paid my rent.'

'Yeah, you have. I came to tell you I'm going back to the States.'

He was surprised at how disappointed he felt that she showed no great reaction. 'For good?' she asked.

'No. A week, ten days, something like that.'

'Why are you telling me? Do you want payment now for the time you're going to be away?'

At that moment Jay admired her more than he'd ever admired any woman. 'I think that can wait until I get back. It merely seemed polite to tell you.'

'Fine, you've told me, now I know.'

She was making him uncomfortable and he couldn't understand why. He was always in control, yet even in a courtroom cross-examining a difficult witness he'd never felt this awkward; her attitude wasn't at all what he'd expected. 'You'll be all right?'

She looked as astonished to hear him say the words as he was to hear himself utter them. 'What's it to you?'

'It was a stupid thing to say. If you need anything from the main house then go to Todd. Pattie isn't exactly well disposed towards you at the moment. She thinks we were alone for too long last night.'

Davina's reply was swift. 'I'd rather not talk about last night.'

'Suits me,' he said fervently.

Davina started to close the door. 'Phil's coming for the weekend tomorrow so I won't be lonely. Please don't worry about me,' she said with mock sweetness.

'I don't know why I bothered to come and tell you,' said Jay, feeling more uncomfortable by the minute.

'Nor do I. Are you going back to the States for work or play?'

'Work. I do all my playing here right now, as I'd have thought you'd realised.'

'I don't know anything about you,' said Davina flatly and closed the door in his face.

Back in his study Jay felt totally frustrated. He couldn't wait to get back to the States, putting England and Davina Fletcher in particular behind him. Work had always been the most important thing in his life. Davina had threatened to change the balance of things but he was certain that once he was the other side of the Atlantic his life would return to normal. All the same, every time he remembered the way she'd clasped her legs round him and he'd thrust into her so vigorously the previous night, he felt himself stir again. His natural honesty forced him to admit to himself that forgetting Davina was going to be more difficult than he was trying to pretend.

'We can't do it here!' exclaimed Phil as Pattie clambered over the passenger seat and onto the back seat of his car.

'Why not?' She seemed surprised.

'Because someone might see us.'

'This lay-by's pretty secluded and there isn't room for another car. What are you worried about?'

'I can't do it anyway,' explained Phil awkwardly. 'I'll be seeing Davina in fifteen minutes.'

'So? You don't have to tell her about this. You don't know how much I've been longing to see you,' purred Pattie.

Phil had been longing to see Pattie too, but he wasn't going to say so. He was too worried about what would happen if she decided to tell Jay.

'Come on,' she urged him. 'Look, I haven't got anything on under my skirt,' and she pulled up the microscopic piece of material that he supposed she was referring to. Beneath it she was totally naked. Her long tanned legs were fully exposed to him, as was the soft golden down of her pubic hair. She sprawled on the back seat moving one hand lazily between her slender thighs and her eyes started to glaze. 'Hurry! Don't you want me?'

'Of course I want you.'

'Then get in the back with me.'

Realising that he wasn't going to keep Pattie's interest by remaining thoroughly English and cautious, Phil opened the driver's door and got into the back. Almost before he'd closed the door behind him her fingers were fumbling at his belt, unfastening it before pulling down his zipper. Immediately his erection sprang through the opening in his boxer shorts.

Pattie gave a squeal of pleasure. 'There, I knew you wanted it as much as I did. You look good enough to eat.' Bending her head she took him into her mouth while at the same time running the fingers of her right hand up and down the stem of his erection until he could feel his testicles drawing up tightly beneath him.

'Careful or I'll come,' he cautioned her.

Hastily Pattie removed her mouth and then pulled her feet up onto the seat, spreading her knees wide apart and opening herself up to him. 'Don't you want to touch?' she asked teasingly.

Phil groaned and then fell on her, his fingers sliding inside her. She was very damp and within a couple of minutes, as he moved his fingers around inside her while rubbing at her clitoris with his other hand, she came, and he felt her internal muscles tighten around his fingers in pulsating contractions.

'Now I want you inside me,' she muttered. He spread himself over her, his feet jammed awkwardly in the space behind the driver's seat. It was like being an adolescent again but that only increased the excitement, giving the whole affair an added urgency. As he started to move his hips, his hands grasped her breasts through the thin strappy T-shirt she was wearing and he squeezed the perfectly sculpted flesh.

Pattie was squealing even louder now, bucking furiously beneath him, and suddenly he felt that he was losing control. 'I'm sorry, I'm coming,' he cried.

'Me too,' squealed Pattie, and almost immediately he felt her tighten around him as her muscles spasmed and she cried out in an ecstasy of delighted abandonment. 'Gee, that was great!' she enthused. 'You Brits are terrific once you let your hair down.'

Phil felt suddenly awkward. 'I wish we could do it somewhere where we had more room, and more time.'

'This was fine. I like a quickie.'

He felt slightly deflated. 'So do I, but I'd love to have more time with you.'

'You will have,' she promised him. 'Jay's gone back to the States for a few days. We've got the whole weekend ahead of us.'

'But what about Davina?' he asked.

'You don't want to worry about Davina,' said Pattie

as the pair of them got back into the front of the car and Phil pulled out of the lay-by. 'She hasn't been faithful to you while you've been away.'

Phil couldn't believe his ears. 'What do you mean?'

'I mean she's been having a good time, like you and I had a good time just now.'

'With Jay?'

Pattie gave a gurgle of laughter. 'With all of us, honey, with all of us.'

Phil looked at her in astonishment and nearly drove into a ditch. 'I don't believe you.'

'I don't care if you believe me or not. Ask her tonight. She doesn't tell you lies, does she?'

'I don't know,' confessed Phil, wondering if the whole world had gone mad. 'She's been a bit odd lately, but ...'

'By lately do you mean since Jay arrived?'

Phil nodded. 'Yes.'

'Then work it out for yourself.'

'But she resents him. He's taken what was rightfully hers, he ...'

'Are you sure Davina's really that worried about her inheritance?' asked Pattie. 'Seems to me you're the one who resents Jay. I can tell you one thing for sure, Jay's got the hots for Davina.'

'I can't imagine that man having "the hots" for anyone,' said Phil crossly. 'It's not in his nature.'

'It wasn't,' admitted Pattie, 'but he's changed. Not that I mind,' she added, running the long fingernails of her right hand up the inside of Phil's left thigh and scratching lightly at his crotch until he began to tremble. 'I think perhaps I'm turning into an Anglophile.'

'For God's sake stop doing that or we'll have an accident,' said Phil. 'Look, I'd better drop you off here. You can walk the last bit, can't you?'

Pattie laughed. 'What's the matter? Are you afraid Davina's going to be annoyed if she thinks you've given me a lift? I tell you, honey, after what's been going on while you've been away she's not going to make trouble about anything. She's going to keep quiet and hope you don't ask too many questions.'

'I'd still prefer you to walk,' said Phil regretfully. 'I don't want to start the weekend off badly.'

'Okay.' She was clearly not fazed in the least by his lack of nerve. 'When am I going to see you again?'

'I don't know.' He wished that he did, wished that he

could arrange a meeting now so that he had something to look forward to, but he couldn't think how it would be possible to get away from Davina.

'Leave it to me,' said Pattie, leaning over and kissing him full on the mouth before getting out of the car. 'I'll think of something.' Phil drove on, watching in his driving mirror as she grew smaller and smaller. He hoped that she was right. Sex with her was far more exciting than it ever was with Davina.

Usually when he arrived on the Saturday morning Davina would be waiting to greet him at the cottage door, but this morning there was no sign of her. He had to ring twice before she even realised he was there, and when he stepped into the hall she kissed him on the cheek in such a casual manner that he could have been her brother rather than her lover.

'Anything wrong?' he asked.

Davina shook her head. 'No, why?'

'It's not much of a welcome that's all.'

'Oh, I'm sorry, perhaps I'm a bit tired.'

'Been busy working?' he asked.

Davina nodded. 'There's a lot of intricate work involved, that's always tiring.'

Phil was certain she was lying. He was no fool; he knew that things had been changing between them ever since Jay's arrival but today she seemed positively indifferent to him. 'Not missing Jay, are you?' He couldn't keep a note of sarcasm out of his voice.

'How do you mean, missing him?'

'Well, he's away in the States and ...'

'How do you know that?' Her eyes were sharp.

Phil could have bitten his tongue off. 'You told me over the phone,' he muttered lamely.

'I most certainly did not. You've been talking to Pattie, haven't you? When?'

'She was on her way out as I drove through the main gates. I stopped and exchanged a few words. She mentioned it then.'

'Why pretend I told you?'

Phil was thrown on the defensive. 'I got muddled.'

Davina glanced out of the lounge window. 'You certainly did. If Pattie was on her way out as you drove in she didn't go very far. She's coming back now. I wonder where she's been?' Before Phil could say anything Davina had opened the window. 'Hi, Pattie! Did you go to the post-box?'

Pattie shook her head. 'I've been for a long run. I'll probably go to the post-box later if you need me to take any letters for you.'

Davina shook her head. 'That's all right, thanks. You've already been very helpful.'

'I have?' Phil could understand the American girl's bewilderment.

'Well?' demanded Davina, turning sharply on her heel and facing him once more. 'Are you going to tell me that she was setting off on this long run only three minutes ago?'

'I don't see why I've got to explain anything to you,' said Phil. 'From what I hear you haven't exactly been a paragon of virtue yourself.'

'I don't know when you talked to Pattie,' said Davina slowly, 'but she certainly seems to have shared a lot of information. Look, Phil, I know you're keen on her and there's no point in pretending you're not. I don't mind. I've got to be honest, things aren't the same between us any more and she's very attractive. The thing is, I'm not very keen on being used.'

'Used?' Phil couldn't believe his ears. 'I'm the one who's been used. I've been coming down here at weekends, sharing your bed and helping you through the loss of your uncle, then the moment my back's turned you're off screwing that American guy. Talk about irony. First he screws you metaphorically over the house, then you literally screw him.'

Davina looked shocked. 'That's a horrible way of talking. Anyway, he didn't "screw" me over the house as you put it. Uncle David left it to him, and he was perfectly entitled to do so.'

'You're not denying you've been sleeping with him, are you?'

Davina shook her head. 'No.'

'I knew it when I saw the pair of you in London.'

'I didn't know you'd seen us.'

'You're not the only one who can keep a secret.'

'What are we going to do?' asked Davina.

Phil sat down. 'I do like Pattie, but I'm hardly in the same league as Jay Prescott, am I? I don't think there's any more chance of her agreeing to marry me than there is of Jay wanting to marry you. All the same, I'd like a chance to see her for a bit longer. Suppose I sleep in the spare room on the weekends?'

'What if Jay finds out?' asked Davina.

Phil felt suddenly angry. 'I don't think he can say much considering the fact he's been having it off with my girlfriend, do you?'

'I'm not sure it's that important to him,' said Davina casually.

'What do you mean?'

'I mean that they have a very open relationship. They're all the same. They seem to believe in complete sexual freedom, even within marriage.'

'You mean Todd and Tanya screw around?'

Davina frowned. 'It sounds horrible when you say it like that.'

'What other way is there of saying it?'

'They enjoy experimental sex,' explained Davina. 'It's difficult to be that experimental when there are only two of you, so naturally from time to time they ...'

Phil couldn't believe his ears. 'You haven't been doing it with all of them, have you?'

Davina shook her head. 'Of course not,' she said quickly. 'Surely you know me better than that?'

'I'm beginning to think I don't know you at all.'

'That makes two of us,' she muttered.

Later, as he unpacked in the spare room, Phil wondered whether he'd been wise to put his cards on the table quite this soon. It was true that Pattie had promised to arrange meetings for them over the weekend, and now he wouldn't have to worry about making excuses to Davina. However, once Jay returned or Pattie tired of him, Phil would be left with nothing. He was still secretly clinging to the hope that eventually the Americans would return to their own country, leaving Davina free to live in the main house. Until this morning he'd fully intended to be at her side when this happened. Now he'd blown all chances of that, but when he thought of Pattie his pulse quickened and he realised that if it all went wrong he'd have no one to blame but himself. He was the victim of his own lust for the gorgeous Californian blonde.

'I can't believe it,' said Tanya to Todd, climbing into bed the following Friday night. 'I was sure Jay would be back tomorrow. What reason did he give for staying on in the States?'

'Work.'

'I don't believe him, do you?'

Todd shook his head. 'Not entirely. At first I wondered if he'd got wind of the fact that Pattie had spent the whole of last weekend making love to Phil, but I doubt if that's the reason. Firstly Pattie wouldn't have been stupid enough to tell him and secondly he doesn't care enough for her for it to matter.'

'Then what is it?'

'I think you know,' said Todd.

'He's in love with Davina, isn't he?' said Tanya. 'He's in love with her and he doesn't know what to do about it.'

'He's not comfortable with emotions,' explained Todd. 'He never has been. Bostonians are like that. They believe that revealing emotion shows a lack of breeding.'

'I'm glad you're not from Boston,' giggled Tanya, running her hand down her husband's stomach and fondling his erection.

'So am I. All the same, it's a pity about Jay. He and Davina really suit each other.'

'Why don't we do something drastic then?' suggested Tanya. 'Something so unexpected that Jay would be forced to admit his true feelings.'

'Like what?'

'It involves you,' murmured Tanya, sliding on top of her husband and rubbing her body up and down his until he was groaning with pleasure. 'The thing is, are you brave enough to do what I'm going to suggest?'

'Probably not if it's going to make Jay mad.'

'You're his boss.'

'That's work, this is play. For Christ's sake, let me inside you.'

Tanya shook her head teasingly. 'Not until you promise to do what I ask.' Raising herself up she allowed him inside her for a fraction of a second then lifted herself off so that he was left thrusting his hips upwards, his face twisted with desire.

'All right,' he moaned. 'I'll do it. I'll do anything as long as I can take you now.'

'You promise you won't go back on your word?'

'Yes,' shouted Todd, then he gripped his wife's slim hips and pulled her down hard until she was sitting astride him, his erection buried up to the hilt in her comforting warmth. He used his hands to lift her up and down in a rhythm that suited him, while she angled herself forward a little to gain maximum stimulation.

'Have you any idea how much I love you?' gasped Todd, feeling his orgasm approaching.

'Of course I have,' she said gently. 'And I love you too. That's why I want Jay to be happy. I want everyone to be as happy as us.'

'I don't think that's possible,' he gasped, and then he was spilling himself inside her just as Tanya's head flew back. The tendons of her neck stood out like whipcords as, for a few seconds, she teetered on the brink of orgasm before finally reaching her climax with a moan of delight.

'So what's your plan?' Todd asked her a little later as she lay curled up in his arms. Tanya whispered in his ear and then laughed because, as he listened to her, Todd's previously flaccid penis began to stir.

'It looks as though you're not just going to agree, you're going to enjoy it as well,' she said with a laugh.

'Isn't that allowed?'

'Of course it is,' she assured him. 'It should make it all the more effective.'

'But how do we get the timing right?' Todd asked his wife.

'I'm going to ring Jay tomorrow and say that I think

he ought to come back and see what's happening for himself. Knowing him he won't waste any time. I think we can safely assume he'll be here by Sunday night.'

'Sunday night it is then,' agreed Todd. 'I hope for all our sakes this works.'

'I hope so too,' said Tanya. 'I really like Davina and Jay, and ...'

'I'm just hoping Jay doesn't kill me,' said Todd.

'I won't let that happen,' Tanya promised him. 'Let's face it, Todd, whatever happens, you'll have had a good time.'

'Yeah, and hopefully Davina will too.'

Tanya looked thoughtful. 'You'll have to coax her, Todd. It isn't the sort of thing that will come naturally to her.'

'You can leave all that to me,' Todd reassured her. 'If there's one thing I do know about it's coaxing women to help them discover the full extent of their sexuality.'

'True,' conceded Tanya and then, finally content, she forgot about Jay and Davina and turned her attentions to her husband once more.

Chapter Twelve

On the Sunday evening Davina prowled restlessly around her cottage. She felt lonely and depressed. Phil had driven back to London, but in some ways that was a relief because she'd scarcely seen him during his visit. When she'd asked him how he and Pattie had enjoyed themselves he'd hesitated for a moment before saying, 'She's fantastic, the most incredible woman I've ever met.' The result had been to make Davina feel totally inadequate. Not only had Jay deserted her, it now seemed that she'd never, even at the beginning, satisfied Phil in the way that Pattie could.

She was beginning to wonder if Jay was ever going to return. Even if he did, she couldn't understand how their relationship could progress. After their last session of lovemaking, when she'd been certain that he'd felt as much for her as she did for him, what more could she do to move the relationship on? It seemed, she conceded to herself, that she'd been wrong about him. He really wasn't the kind of man who was ever going to settle down. Although he'd taught her a lot about sex, she'd been stupid to read more into it than that.

There was plenty of work waiting for her in the studio, but she wasn't in the mood for work. After the experiences of the past few weeks she found that she was shamefully obsessed with sex. Her body was now finely tuned to sensual pleasure, and when she was forced to go without sex she missed it in a way that she never had before. Every night, before she could sleep, she had to masturbate. She knew that there was nothing wrong with this but still felt a sense of shame, as though in some way she was a failure because she had no man to make love to her in the way that her body craved.

The ring on the doorbell took her by surprise. Her heart started to pound and she ran to open it, convinced that Jay must have returned without her knowledge. When she saw Todd standing on the doorstep her heart sank. 'Oh, it's you.'

'You don't sound very pleased to see me.'

She felt guilty. 'I'm sorry, I was expecting someone else.'

'Jay?' he asked.

All at once Davina had to tell someone the truth. 'Yes,' she said miserably. 'I thought you were Jay,' and to her horror she felt her eyes full with tears.

'Hey, you mustn't cry, honey,' said Todd. 'Here, let's try and talk this thing through.'

Davina took him into the front room and the pair of them sat side by side on the sofa. There, with the late evening sun slanting through the windows, Davina confessed her feelings about Jay and her desolation now that she was beginning to realise he didn't feel the same about her.

'You could be wrong,' said Todd when she'd finished talking. 'Tanya and I think he does care for you. We believe that's why he's run off, because he can't face his own feelings.'

'Well, if he can't face up to them there's no point in him having them,' replied Davina. 'Even if you're right, he's never going to admit it to me. I wish I'd never met him.'

'Hey, that's not true and you know it. If you'd never met him you'd never have met any of us. We've had some good times, haven't we?'

Davina nodded. 'Yes, but . . .'

'I know, we're not Jay, but you've enjoyed the sex and so have we. We've also taught you to loosen up a bit, which can't be bad.'

Davina managed a weak smile. 'I suppose that's true.'

She didn't quite know how it happened but suddenly Todd's right arm was round her shoulders and his left hand was lightly stroking her thigh through the material of her skirt. 'If I weren't a happily married man, I'd sure as hell marry you,' he murmured. 'You're incredibly sexy. I even dream about you.'

'Do you really?' asked Davina curiously.

Todd nodded. 'Yep. I've told Tanya about it. Luckily our relationship's so stable it doesn't trouble her. Truth to tell, I don't think she's surprised, you see we don't get women like you in America.'

'Which is presumably why Jay's fled back there.'

Todd shook his head. 'Not necessarily' He tilted her towards him a little and began to kiss her lightly on the corners of her mouth while at the same time his hand continued its insidiously arousing caress, only this time his fingers moved beneath her skirt until they reached the soft silken skin at the top of her hold-up stockings. It felt delicious and his kiss was so tender, so relaxing, that Davina didn't attempt to stop him. 'I know you love Jay,' muttered Todd, 'but that doesn't mean we can't have some fun together, does it?'

Davina shook her head. Why should she miss out on this, she thought to herself, simply because Jay wasn't able to deal with his emotions. 'I'll draw the curtains,' continued Todd. Once they were safe from prying eyes he carefully removed her skirt and blouse leaving her standing in her white bra and matching French knickers. 'You've got lovely skin,' he whispered, standing behind her and running the tip of his tongue over the vertebrae at the top of her spine. 'So white and creamy. You're a real English rose.'

Davina gave a sigh of contentment. Her flesh was tingling with excitement and as Todd sat her down on the sofa, his hands roaming all over her body, she felt her breasts begin to swell. Todd quickly undressed and then sat on the floor at her feet, stretching one leg upwards so that his toes were between her thighs. Then he began to use his big toe to massage her through the crotch of her panties, and her belly ached and tightened as her excitement mounted.

She could feel the material sticking to her as her juices began to flow. She couldn't believe how skilful he was and let her head fall against the back of the sofa so that she could concentrate on the incredible sensations he was arousing. The pressure was firm, the movements circular and steady, and her excited clitoris swelled until her whole body tensed in preparation for release. To her horror Todd suddenly removed his foot.

Davina's eyes flew open and she stared down at him. 'I don't want to delay it, I was just about to come then.'

'Sure, but it'll be better if you wait a little while. How about you do something for me now?'

They swapped places and Davina knelt on the floor while he sat on the edge of the sofa as she drew his erection into her mouth, flicking at the tip with her tongue before moving her head up and down the shaft until he began to groan and pulled himself out of her.

Now they changed positions once more, only this time he removed her panties first and then began to nibble the smooth flesh of her inner thighs before sliding his thumb between her damp inner sex lips. Frantically she lifted the cheeks of her bottom off the sofa trying to get him to touch her clitoris but he pushed her back down. 'Wait,' he commanded. 'You mustn't be in such a hurry.'

'Please let me come,' she begged him.

'I will, but not yet.'

Now he used both fingers and tongue to tease the whole swollen area. His tongue moved around her clitoris with lazy circular movements while his fingers continued to roam over the damp flesh. Then, as her body trembled violently, he carefully closed her outer sex lips and pressed his mouth over her pubic mound in a strangely intimate caress that increased the hot pressure deep within her without offering her any chance of release.

'I can't stand it any longer,' she whimpered, ashamed of her own need but desperate.

'Not much longer,' he promised, turning his attention towards her breasts. Now his tongue was drawing lazy circles around her nipples, his teeth occasionally nipping at the rock-hard tips while his hands moved lightly over the flesh that covered her ribcage before he palpated her slightly rounded belly, swollen with desire.

The result was an increase in the pressure that was building up deep within her, somewhere behind her pelvic bone, and she felt that if she wasn't allowed to climax soon she'd explode. She was making strange keening noises now, writhing desperately on the sofa, her head moving from side to side, while he continued his incredibly skilful torment that was giving her such delicious bittersweet pleasure.

'Okay,' he whispered against her ear. 'I think you've waited long enough now. Spread your thighs wider apart.'

Almost weeping with gratitude she did as he asked and his mouth travelled down her body, kissing her breasts, waist and belly before at last he was once more between her thighs. This time he drew her clitoris into his mouth and sucked rhythmically on it. For a couple of seconds the dreadful full feeling increased but finally the first pulsating throbs began behind her clitoris and then her body was racked by a huge orgasm, an orgasm so intense that she nearly lost consciousness.

'Didn't I tell you it would be worth waiting for?' asked Todd as she lay gasping on the sofa.

Davina nodded weakly. It had been fantastic, but despite the pleasure there was a hollowness about it all because skilled as Todd was, caring as he was, she wasn't in love with him. He could bring her body to heights of ecstasy but, no matter how much she tried to fool herself, there was something missing.

'Let's go upstairs,' said Todd. 'I think we should continue this in the bedroom.'

Davina hesitated. She wasn't certain that she wanted to carry on. Todd gave her a lazy smile and lightly cupped her breasts in his hands. 'Come on,' he urged her. 'Let's try something different. You're capable of having lots more orgasms you know.'

'Why do we have to go upstairs?'

'Because we need the bed,' explained Todd.

Davina knew that if she chose to send Todd away, she'd regret it later. Tonight she'd once again lie alone in her bed, and once more she'd almost certainly end up pleasuring herself. She liked Todd, and it was clear he liked her. There seemed no point in longing for Jay when he'd gone off to the States in order to forget her.

'Come on,' urged Todd. 'You'll surprise yourself.'

Throwing caution to the wind, Davina nodded. Once inside her bedroom she lay down on the bed waiting for Todd to join her, but instead he began rummaging through the drawers of her dressing table. 'What do you want?' she asked.

'Some scarves.'

'Why?'

'So that I can tie you up.'

He sounded completely matter-of-fact, as though there was nothing unusual about what he was saying, but Davina's heart quickened and she shook her head. 'I don't think I'd like that.'

'Sure you would. Tell you what, if you want me to untie you at any time just say. You trust me, don't you?'

'I suppose so,' she conceded.

Todd looked hurt. 'Surely you do. I'm a friend of Jay's, I'd never do anything to hurt you. Pattie and Tanya love this kind of sex. It will really add something extra for you.'

Davina showed him where she kept her scarves and

then nervously raised her arms above her head so that he could fasten her wrists to the bedstead. He fetched extra pillows from another room so that her head was well raised. 'Comfortable?' Davina nodded. 'Great. Then I can begin.'

Davina waited tensely. Already, despite her fear, she was becoming aroused and she trembled as Todd fetched a third scarf, a long narrow silk one and began to draw it over her skin. He used it to surround each breast, lifting it slightly and then lowering it, teasing at the rapidly burgeoning nipple with a corner of the material so that she squirmed helplessly with the sheer pleasure of it.

He spent a long time sliding the silk scarf over her upper torso before moving it lower down her, but not where she wanted it. Instead, he ran it from side to side across each of her insteps and then drew it in and out of the spaces between her toes. Soon she could feel her hips start to twitch as her body searched for greater stimulation, in order to bring about the satisfaction she so desperately craved.

'You're very responsive,' whispered Todd. 'I guessed you would be.'

'Touch me between my thighs,' Davina begged him, but he shook his head.

'Not yet, honey. That's why you're tied up. This way I can control exactly when you get touched there. Right now I've got plenty more in mind before that happens.'

Davina groaned.

Todd looked down at her for a moment and then vanished from the room. She realised that he was going downstairs and when he returned saw that he was carrying a large plastic tumbler full of ice cubes. Her flesh felt hot, as though she was on fire, and when he lazily moved one of the ice cubes over her left nipple her whole body went rigid with shock. The contrast between the hot blood coursing through her veins and the slowly melting ice was incredible. Her nerve endings leapt with desire and once more she lifted her lower body upwards, frantic for him to touch her where she most needed it.

Todd no longer bothered to talk to her. Even when she pleaded with him for some relief from the terrible aching between her thighs he ignored her. He sucked on the ice cubes himself before fastening his mouth around her breasts, and the coolness made her gasp. After that, he held an ice cube up in the air and as she watched, mesmerised, he slowly lowered it, until finally he dropped it into her bellybutton and she whimpered as she felt it start to melt. Tiny cool rivulets of water began to run down her stomach and into the creases at the top of her thighs, but no matter how much she tried to manipulate her body none of it would go between her sex lips.

Davina began to pull at her bonds. 'You've got to touch me or let me touch myself,' she shouted.

'That would ruin the whole point of tying you up.'

'I don't want to be tied up any more.'

'Gee, that's too bad.'

Davina couldn't believe her ears. 'You said you'd untie me if I asked you to.'

'Did I? Sorry, I didn't mean it.'

For the first time Davina saw how stupid she'd been. After all, what did she know about Todd? She thought she liked and trusted him, but they were alone in the cottage with no Tanya or Pattie to keep an eye on things. His erection was huge and briefly he lay on top of her, moving himself up and down and stimulating the shaft of his erection against her pubic bone. This had the effect of increasing her desperate need for an orgasm as her whole body swelled and tightened. Then, at the precise moment that the first rhythmic pulsations started, he moved off her and casually ran a hand over her quaking lower belly.

'Hey, you really are close to coming, aren't you?'

Swiftly she jerked her hips up, hoping that the brief moment of contact with his hand would be sufficient to trigger her climax but his reactions were faster than hers and he moved his hand away. 'Naughty!' he reproved her and suddenly he flicked hard at each of her nipples in turn, causing them to sting and burn. Davina cried out in protest but she realised that the sensation had only increased her desire. She could feel the moisture seeping out of her between her thighs, and her sex lips swelling and parting.

'Let's see how you're getting on,' murmured Todd and at last she felt his fingers probe the delicate, aroused flesh. He touched her gently, his manner almost detached. Then he swirled a finger round the entrance to her vagina and spread some of her own moisture upwards in one brief touch that caressed her clitoris for a fleeting instant. The caress was bliss, hot pleasure seared through her, but the stimulation was too brief to allow her to come and she sobbed with frustration.

Todd continued to torment her with the silk scarf and the ice cubes until her excitement was so great, her need so incredible, that she could tell he was in danger of coming himself. Apparently sensing this, he knelt over her upper body. Pushing her breasts up and in he trapped his straining erection between them and began to move his hips. 'You don't mind if I come, do you?' he asked.

'What about me?' she wailed.

'I think I'm gonna make you wait another hour or so.'

'Please, please don't do this to me,' she sobbed. 'This isn't what I wanted, this isn't what I thought it would be like. Please let me go.'

Suddenly the bedroom door crashed open. 'What the hell do you think you're doing?' shouted Jay, and turning her head Davina saw him framed in the doorway, his eyes dark with rage. 'Get off her, Todd.'

'Hang in there, I'm just about to come,' said Todd calmly.

Crossing the room in two strides Jay grabbed hold of

his friend by his right arm and pulled him off the tethered Davina. 'Did you hear what I said? Get out of this cottage now, before I kill you.'

Davina was bewildered by Todd's reaction. He didn't seem nearly as frightened as she was and although he began to leave the room he seemed surprised by what was happening, surprised and displeased. 'What are you in such a state about, Jay? You were in the States, Davina was missing the sex and I provided it. What's wrong with that?'

'You and Tanya were my guests,' snapped Jay. 'You've abused my hospitality. This cottage is Davina's, not mine.'

'But Davina invited me in.'

Jay looked at Davina and she struggled frantically, trying to free her wrists. 'I did,' she confessed. 'But I never wanted this to happen.'

'You mean he tied you up against your will?'

'No, but . . . '

'There, what did I tell you,' said Todd complacently.

'Damn you, just get out,' yelled Jay. 'I want you and Tanya gone by morning. I'm not kidding either, do you understand me?'

'Sure.' Todd sounded perfectly equable about the whole thing. 'We'll go back to the States. I don't want to outstay my welcome. What are you doing back here anyway? I thought you were needed in Boston?'

'That's none of your business. Now go.'

Davina heard Todd's footsteps on the stairs and a few minutes later the front door closed behind him. 'Please untie me,' she whispered to Jay as he stood staring down at her.

She was certain that he was going to but at the last moment he hesitated and, walking to the foot of the bed, put a hand between her thighs. 'He's turned you on,' he said accusingly. 'You're soaking wet.'

'He was doing nice things,' whispered Davina. 'It just got out of control.'

'How could you?' asked Jay incredulously. 'Do you mean you like being taken against your will?'

'It wasn't like that. He said he'd release me whenever I wanted and then he wouldn't.'

'Doesn't seem to have stopped you wanting him,' said Jay, his voice deep with desire. Davina opened her mouth to reply but before she could say anything his fingers were gliding over her frantic flesh. He finally touched her where she'd been longing for Todd to touch her, and all the pent-up sexual tension that had been driving her out of her mind was released as he lightly massaged the area around her clitoris.

With a groan she felt her climax sweep over her and the delicious ripples of pleasure spread through her whole body. Before she'd even finished Jay was on top of her, fumbling at his trousers and freeing his erection. With no preliminaries and still fully clothed he thrust violently into her, his hands gripping her sore, abused breasts, but his touch was light. As he moved inexorably towards his own orgasm he licked and sucked at her breasts and to her delight, as he came, a second climax rushed through her. She shuddered beneath him, calling out his name in ecstasy.

When it was over he remained slumped on top of her for a few minutes before reluctantly rolling off and unfastening her wrists. He rubbed the aching skin before putting his mouth to each of her wrists in turn and kissing them lightly, his tongue flicking into the palm of her hand in an incredibly erotic movement that, despite all that had gone before, made her body stir once more.

'You had no right to ask him in here,' he muttered, pulling her against him.

Davina felt very safe wrapped in his arms but anger flared through her at his words. 'You've no right to tell me who I can have here,' she retorted, moving away from him. 'I pay my rent. Don't tell me you want to vet my guest list as well as collecting bizarre forms of payment.'

'Of course I don't want to vet everyone who comes in and out of the cottage. I'm just saying that what you did was stupid.'

'Even if it was, what's it to you? As far as I knew you were in the States.'

'And that gives you the right to do what you like?'

Davina couldn't believe what she was hearing. 'I've always had the right to do what I like. You don't own me or control me, Jay. You're my landlord, that's all.'

Jay grasped her chin between his thumb and forefinger. 'Is that really all?'

'I don't know what you mean,' she lied.

Abruptly he released her. 'Then there's no point in me saying any more. I must say that if nothing else I'm gratified that I've managed to free you of all your sexual inhibitions. You should have seen what you looked like when I came into the room just now.'

'It was because I was missing you,' Davina blurted out.

Jay looked hard at her. 'Was it really? Gee, I hate to think what might happen when I go back to the States then. I guess I'd better take you with me as my wife.'

'Excuse me?' Davina wanted to be sure that she'd heard him right.

'I said, I guess I'd better take you back with me to the States when I go, as my wife.'

He wasn't smiling at her, his eyes weren't even soft, and Davina couldn't believe that this was a genuine proposal of marriage. She was convinced that it was another of his tests. If she refused he'd throw her out of the cottage saying that he couldn't have her living so near when she'd turned down his proposal. If she accepted he wouldn't be able to throw her out, but she wondered how he would react. 'I can't think of anything I'd like better,' she said with a smile.

To her amazement he didn't reel back in horror. In fact, for the first time ever, a look of delight crossed his face and his eyes were bright with excitement. 'Do you really mean it? In spite of all that's happened and all you know about me, you're willing to be my wife? I think I'd better be honest with you about a few things. The wife of a prosecutor in Boston has a very set role to play. You'll be able to do it, I've no fears about that, but the conventions might irritate you at first.'

'I'm a very conventional girl, or was,' Davina reminded him. 'I think I'll be able to handle that.'

'You're not kidding me, are you?' he asked, and it was the first time that she'd ever heard him sound unsure. 'You really do want to marry me?'

It was only then that Davina understood that he was telling the truth, and that he did want to marry her. The fact that he hadn't told her he loved her, or talked about his feelings for her, didn't matter. She realised that he wasn't that kind of a man, but she had to feel free to tell him how she felt. 'There's something you ought to know,' she said softly.

He looked anxious. 'What?'

'That I'm in love with you. I know that to you that's a word that's forbidden but it's how I feel. It isn't just a sexual thing between us, I know that for certain now. It was good with Todd, until we got upstairs, but I still felt hollow and empty, as though something was missing. What was missing was emotional commitment, or love as I call it. This wouldn't be a business arrangement for me, Jay. I see now what my uncle was trying to tell me. I never loved Phil, not in the way that I love you. You're in my thoughts all the time, I can't think of anything else, not even my work. You have to know this, in case you want a more detached wife.'

'A more detached wife? Is that how you think I feel about you?' he asked incredulously. 'Hell, I haven't been able to get you out of my mind either. I thought once I was back in the States I could forget all about you but it didn't work. Do you want to know why I came back tonight?'

'Yes.'

'Because Tanya called me and told me that she was worried Todd was getting too keen on you. She said the pair of you were spending hours alone here in the cottage day after day. I've never known such jealousy as I felt then. I caught the first plane I could back here and when I got to the house Tanya told me that the pair of you were here, which is why I burst in on you like that.'

Davina opened her mouth to tell him that she and

Todd hadn't been spending endless days together, that tonight had been their first time, but then she changed her mind. She realised that Todd and Tanya must have plotted this in order to make Jay confront his feelings, and felt a surge of affection and gratitude towards them. Without their help she doubted if Jay would ever have admitted how he felt to himself let alone her. 'What about Pattie?' she asked.

'Yeah, I've been thinking about her. She ain't gonna be heartbroken. Sure, she wanted to be a Bostonian wife, but I can't see it, can you?' He laughed.

'Not really,' agreed Davina.

'In any case, from what I hear she and Phil are an item now. Since you and I will be in the States a lot of the time, I thought we'd leave them in charge of the house and cottage. That should make Phil happy. He seems to think he should have inherited it in the first place. That way it will always be ready for us when we want to return.'

'Have you mentioned this to Pattie?'

'Nope, not yet. I'll talk to her this evening.'

'You're very confident that you can arrange other people's lives, aren't you?'

Jay shook his head. 'Not any more. It's a pity about Todd, he and I were good friends but . . . '

'Why can't you stay friends?' asked Davina. 'He wasn't doing anything wrong. You'd have behaved in exactly the same way. He wasn't to know how you felt about me, unless you'd said something to him.'

Jay shook his head. 'I never admitted it to myself, so I certainly wouldn't have admitted it to Todd.'

'Then you can't really blame him, can you? All of you have spent your lives having sex with each other whenever you felt like it, and as long as it was simply fun nobody got hurt. How was Todd expected to know that this was different?'

'I guess you're right, but it's gonna take me a while to get over what I saw.'

'What happens now?' queried Davina.

'I guess I've got some sorting out to do back at the house. Oh yeah, I forgot to tell you, I've got another month here and then my sabbatical's over. Something's come up which means that we'll be leaving by the beginning of September. Is that okay?' he added.

Davina laughed. 'You see, it isn't that difficult thinking about other people's feelings as well, is it?'

He gave a wry grin. 'I'm sure I'll get used to it.'

'Don't worry,' said Davina, resting her head against his chest. 'Early September sounds fine to me.'

On the first Saturday in September, Davina and Jay walked out of the church where Davina's Uncle David had been buried, the church where she'd first set eyes on Jay, as husband and wife. The wedding had been a very low-key affair, with less than a dozen guests because of the haste with which it had had to be arranged. Davina wasn't bothered. She was more fulfilled and self-confident now than she'd ever been, and had no fears about her ability to be a good wife to Jay. After the reception at the house she went upstairs to the master bedroom where so many extraordinary things had happened to her during the summer and began to change into her going-away outfit. As she was dressing, Tanya came into the room.

'You look great, honey,' she exclaimed, looking at Davina's cream suit with its ankle-length pencil skirt and the jacket that fitted at the waist and then flared over her hips. 'Jay's a lucky guy, but I think he knows that.'

'I'm lucky too,' said Davina. 'Never, in my wildest dreams, had I imagined meeting a man like him. I know it's not going to be easy in the States, but Jay's promised that if it all gets too much for me we'll come back here and retreat from the rat race, recharge our batteries as it were.'

'In Boston you'll have to live a conventional life,' Tanya cautioned her.

Davina nodded. 'I know, Jay's already warned me. Leading a conventional life doesn't seem to have stopped him having fun with you and Todd though.'

'You just have to be careful,' explained Tanya.

'Pattie and Phil are happy too,' said Davina. 'I sometimes think this house means more to Phil than it does to me. How about Jay and Todd? Are they getting on all right again?'

Tanya nodded. 'Yeah, although Jay's still a bit cool with Todd. We don't mind. He must never ever guess that we set the whole thing up, that would ruin everything.'

'Don't worry, I won't tell him.'

Tanya kissed Davina lightly on the cheek. 'I know we'll be meeting up again in America, but until then have a great time and remember, no matter how detached he seems, Jay really is madly in love with you.'

Ten minutes later Jay and Davina were driving to the airport where they were to catch a plane for their Caribbean honeymoon. 'You're quiet,' said Jay, putting his hand on her thigh. 'Not having second thoughts already, I hope?'

'Of course not. I was thinking about something Tanya said to me.'

'Oh yeah, what was that?'

'She kept going on about how careful I'd have to be in Boston. She was emphasising what a conventional life we'd have to lead once we're settled over there.'

Jay laughed. 'Sure, we have to be outwardly conventional, but in the privacy of our bedroom we can do exactly what we like.'

'You mean we'll still go on seeing Todd and Tanya?'

'Maybe not Todd and Tanya, but I've got other friends and I know you'll like them. Don't worry, Davina. I haven't finished expanding your horizons yet.'

Davina leant back against the headrest with a sigh of

contentment. 'I'm very glad to hear it. Sometimes I wonder what you've done to me.'

'It doesn't really matter what I've done to you,' Jay pointed out. 'The question is, are you happy with the new you?'

'Oh yes,' said Davina enthusiastically. 'I've never been this happy in my life before.'

She closed her eyes, suddenly exhausted by the past few weeks. Even now, watching Jay's hands on the steering wheel she imagined them wandering all over her body, arousing and satisfying her, bringing her to orgasm again and again until she was utterly sated. As desire gripped her she reached out and pressed her hand between his thighs. 'Sometimes I'm afraid that I'm insatiable,' she confessed.

'In that case, I've certainly chosen the right wife,' laughed Jay. 'When we get to our hotel we'll open a bottle of champagne to the memory of your Uncle David. I get the feeling he'd be pretty damned happy with everything that's happened to both of us.'

'I think you're right,' agreed Davina, and with a smile on her lips she fell asleep, lost in a haze of sensual day-dreams about herself, Jay and their future life together.

Once on the plane she put her head on Jay's shoulder. 'Wake me when we get there,' she murmured sleepily.

'Don't worry,' said Jay, 'I will. Do you know the first thing I'm going to do after we've drunk our champagne?'

'What?'

'I'm going to tie you to the bed, the way Todd did that day when I got back from the States, and I'm going to drive you out of your mind with pleasure. How does that sound to you?'

Excitement surged through Davina and to her shame she realised that she was wriggling on her seat. 'Ecstasy,' she said softly, and knew for sure that everything was going to be all right. No matter how much everyone talked about convention, Jay would never change. Together they'd discover even more about themselves and their own sexuality. The prospect was dazzling. 'Thank you, Uncle David,' she whispered beneath her breath, then finally she slept.